Bronte's
Book Club

Bronte's Book Club

BY

Kristiana Gregory

Holiday House / New York

Library of Congress Cataloging-in-Publication Data

Gregory, Kristiana.
Bronte's book club / by Kristiana Gregory. — 1st ed.
p. cm.
Summary: When twelve-year-old Bronte moves to a small California beach town,
her idea to form a book club in order to make friends turns out to be
a good one, after a rocky start.
ISBN-13: 978-0-8234-2136-7 (hardcover)
[1. Book clubs (Discussion groups)—Fiction.   2. Friendship—Fiction.
3. O'Dell, Scott, 1898–1989. Island of the Blue Dolphins—Fiction.
4. California—Fiction.]   I. Title.
PZ7.G8619Br 2008
[Fic]—dc22
2007036806

In 1960, in California, a few of us neighborhood kids started the Manhattan Beach 4th Street Book and Snack Club. That wasn't its official name, but that's how we thought of it. We were nine years old. With younger siblings tagging along, we rode our bikes to the pier then up the hill to the library where whispering—*quiet* whispering—was strictly enforced. There we roamed the stacks until we each found a book to check out, its plastic cover then crackling against our handlebars as we rode home, *fast*, because of the treats that awaited us. It was the best part of the club, eating our snacks while looking out at the ocean. Though we never actually discussed the stories we read, we sure had fun.

In that same spirit of fun, *Bronte* is dedicated to kids everywhere who want to encourage one another to read by starting their own book club.

Contents

Bronte's
Book Club

Chapter 1

Great Expectations

The alarm clock buzzed through the quiet house, reaching into Bronte's sleep. For a moment she thought she was in a motel room with another day of driving ahead. Then she heard the waves.

Her window was open. For several minutes she lay in bed listening to the surf—a wonderful new sound—and then pipes rattling in the walls as Dad began his shower. When she heard classical music, she knew Mom had unpacked the CD player. Bronte got up and wandered into the kitchen. She could smell fresh coffee.

"Vivaldi's *Four Seasons*," she guessed as she hugged her mother. It was a morning ritual they had enjoyed since she was old enough to learn composers' names.

"Correct, my darling."

A jar of crunchy peanut butter was on the counter, ready for Bronte's toast. This was their first full day in Gray's Beach, California. Though it didn't feel like home yet, she hoped it would soon.

"Mom, it's so cool we're finally here. And summer's just begun. I can't believe I'll be walking to the beach!"

"Same here. I think I'm still in shock. Finally, our dream's come true: to live in a town by the sea."

"Do you really think we'll see the gray whales?"

"That's what the realtor told me—this fall when they head south to Mexico."

"Mom, are you scared?"

"About what, dear?"

Bronte glanced out the open front door where there was a view of the pier. A tiny restaurant was out on the end. "It's just weird," she said. "So far all we've seen of this place are pictures on the Internet. We sold practically everything to get here, and now you and Daddy own that little café."

Her mother nodded, taking a slow sip of coffee. She, too, was looking at the ocean. After a moment she set her mug on the counter. "Honey, I unpacked the ice chest from our trip and put everything here in the fridge. There's plenty of fruit and lunch meat. And we'll be on the pier if you need us. Feeling brave enough to explore today?"

"Absolutely, positively! Mom, I'm so done with being a wallflower. In my new opinion, I've decided twelve is entirely too old to be shy. You're going to see the new and improved Bronte Bella. A courageous heart."

Her mother laughed. "That's my girl."

The Bella cottage was white with blue shutters and faced the harbor. Wind chimes made from seashells were clacking in the breeze, and over the front door there was a crown of bright pink bougainvillea that trailed down to a picket fence with a gate.

Bronte opened the gate and walked partway down the road. Sand dunes sloped to the shore. Though it was a cool June morning, already young children were by the water building sand castles. Kids were riding the waves on Boogie boards, and girls about Bronte's age were playing volleyball—in bikinis! They were trim and golden enough to be on the cover of *Teen*. Everyone seemed to be blond.

Bronte had red hair and freckles. She looked down at her plump legs. Her skin was pale from being indoors all winter, and she had never worn a bikini—she didn't even own a two-piece. Living at the beach was going to be different than living in New Mexico, *wretchedly* different. She hurried back into the house.

At noon Bronte was still in her bedroom. She gazed out her window at the blue ocean. A lighthouse stood on a rocky point of land.

Someday I'm gonna go up that thing.

But every time Bronte thought about leaving the front yard—about being among strangers and those California girls—she felt swirly in her stomach. So she changed the subject by unpacking. She hung up posters and arranged her shoes on the floor of the closet according to color and style. Then she organized her books. First she displayed them alphabetically by author, then alphabetically by title. This took two hours. Her copy of *Jane Eyre,* however, had a reserved spot on her nightstand. It was her favorite, *and* her parents had named her after the author, Charlotte Bronte.

At last she was bored. Bronte cranked up a Mozart CD, then stretched out on her bed to read. If her parents hadn't sold their TV, she would have turned that on, too. Good and loud.

She stayed in the house all day.

By the next afternoon Bronte had grown tired of rearranging her books. She was tired of her bedroom and the house and looking out at the bay.

"Fiddlesticks!" she shouted. It was a word her grandpa had said when he was wound up with irritation. It was old-fashioned, but Bronte didn't care. She liked the sound of it. Taking pencil and paper from the kitchen drawer, she wrote a note to her parents, telling them where she was going.

Then she stepped out onto the stone walkway and opened the little white gate. The harbor was colorful with a regatta—sailboats racing among striped buoys. Seagulls cried and soared in the breeze. In the distance Santa Cruz Island was a purple lump on the horizon.

One . . . two . . . three. Bronte took a deep breath of the fresh, salty air, then closed the gate behind her.

Chapter 2

In a Town by the Sea

It took Bronte seven minutes to walk down the hill. Boutiques and surf shops lined the strand, but she couldn't take her eyes off the ocean. It was vast and blue and moving. The breeze was moist, unlike the heat of the desert.

Lonesome for her friends, she watched the waves. *I wish they could see this!*

Finally she went into Davy Jones's Deli. Three girls were at the take-out counter ordering sorbet. They were wearing short shorts with bathing-suit tops. Bronte envied their tans and sun-streaked hair, and especially their beachy flip-flops. The girls' toes were painted pink. One had a toe ring; another had a butterfly tattoo on her ankle.

"Hello," Bronte said, but they ignored her. She

glanced down at her feet. She had never thought to try a pedicure. Her huaraches, thick leather sandals so popular with her friends back home, now seemed horribly, undeniably clunky.

Bronte shoved her hands into her pockets and glared at the overhead menu. *Carrot juice. Fresh melon balls. Tofu salad. Brown rice pudding.* When it was her turn to order, she leaned close to the waitress and spoke in a low voice. "A chocolate milk shake, please. And fries, extra crispy. To go. Thank you very much."

Another girl, about Bronte's age, was sitting at the counter, flipping idly through a book. Bronte craned her neck to see the title so she could brave a conversation. But just then a waitress with the name tag *Dorothy* set a paper sack in front of the girl and tore a ticket from her order pad.

"There you go, Willow," the older woman said. "Say hello to your mom for me. You come back and chat soon."

The girl paid at the register. Willow was perfectly named because she was tall and thin. *And* pretty. Her long, blond hair hung over one shoulder. On her way out the door, she surprised Bronte by smiling at her.

"Oh . . . hi," Bronte responded. "I mean, good-bye. Oh, I mean . . ."

Willow laughed, but not unkindly. "Maybe I'll see you around," she said to Bronte.

The pier was made from planks of wood with narrow spaces in between. Bronte knelt down and put her eye to one of the cracks; and when she saw ripples of dark water far below, she felt a small thrill. It was mysteriously beautiful.

She finished her fries, then passed huddles of fishermen and tourists, the Bait Shop, and a popcorn stand. Gulls along the railing watched for food like vultures, even hopping behind a baby stroller for a dropped cookie.

At the Breakers Café, Bronte was happy to see people outside waiting to be seated. The aroma of charcoal-broiled hamburgers must mean her parents were hard at work. Bronte didn't want to bother them so she found a bench at the very tip of the pier. It was windy out here. She rested her feet on the lower railing and by leaning forward, could see the green swells rolling beneath her toward shore. She imagined being on a ship at sea with nothing in front of her but the wild blue ocean.

Bronte liked the feel of the waves, how each one shook the pilings ever so slightly and left a mist in the air. *I'm going to love it here!*

A wooden sloop in the harbor had just dropped its sails. It was drifting next to a buoy that had a large iron ring on top. A man on board was tying a rope to it while a woman lowered an anchor from the bow. A girl about Bronte's age was helping them. After they had furled the sails and coiled all the loose lines, the girl settled among some cushions with a book.

Bronte sipped her milk shake, finishing it with a long, noisy slurp. This second girl with a book was giving her an idea.

Chapter 3

Getting Ready

That evening at dinner, Bronte was bursting to share her new plan with her parents.

With a flourish she held up a printout from her computer and read aloud:

Attention! GIRLS who like to read!!
Book Club, Wednesdays, 3—5 pm
Bronte Bella's house—308 View Crest Drive
Inquiries: Breakers Café or
surfergirl@lighthouse.com
Refreshments will be served
Dogs Welcome

"What a great idea," said Dad.

Mom said, "I agree completely."

"So it's okay with you?" Bronte asked. "I mean, if I post these around town and we meet here? I'll clean up. Promise."

Her father grinned. "I especially like the idea of dogs joining in on the book discussions."

While waiting for Wednesday, Bronte forced herself out of the house every morning by ten o'clock. Not ready to appear in her one-piece Speedo from swim team, she wore shorts and a tank top for wading. After several days she could no longer resist the cool, salty water and sat right down in the wet sand. Gasping, she let a small wave wash over her legs and shoulders. Its cold, shivery splash delighted her.

"Fantastication!" she shouted. Her grandpa had said this every time he won at cribbage or whenever Bronte had baked his favorite cookies. He had insisted the word was in the dictionary. *Fantastication!* In addition to her friends, she missed Grandpa more than ever.

Early on book club morning, Bronte found a pair of rubber flip-flops by her nightstand with a note from Mom. "Have fun, darling! We love you."

She jumped out of bed, showered, then rummaged through the kitchen. "Every club needs a snack, that's my motto." She penciled a grocery list.

Bronte marched down the hill, arms swinging, her new flip-flops snapping dirt at her ankles. On the strand she stopped to look out at the water. Surfers were sitting astride their boards, bobbing in the glassy swells as they waited for the perfect one to ride.

The air was so still, the small breaking waves sounded like a whispered *shh . . . shh.*

She was the only customer in the market. At the checkout counter she paid for a brownie mix, orange juice, and a box of Happy Pup Yummy Treats. "I'm having a party this afternoon," she told the cashier.

"Whatever."

At one o'clock the brownies were cooling by the kitchen window. In one of the unpacked boxes, she found a colorful Mexican serape, which she spread over the low table in the sunroom, then arranged cups, plates, and napkins. Next to the brownies Bronte set out a dish of dog biscuits, which were shaped like miniature bones. She put a water bowl by the front door.

During the next hour Bronte swept the house, then the steps and patio. She sat down to wait. It was two-thirty. Five minutes later she rushed over to the mirror, miserable about being a redhead with fair, freckled skin. In a fury she brushed her hair into a ponytail, looked at her profile left and right, then yanked out the elastic.

At three o'clock Bronte reorganized the table. Suddenly she saw things through fresh eyes.

Oh, no! Not one dish or cup matched. Everything was a different size and color. The paper napkins were monogrammed with names, such as DAIRY QUEEN and OLLIE'S ALL-RIGHT BURGERS.

Why can't I have normal parents! And for the millionth time in her life, Bronte wished she had a brother or sister to keep her company, and she especially wished for a dog.

Dogs knew how to sympathize.

Chapter 4

Staying Busy

Bronte sat alone in the sunroom. It was half past three.

She looked out the window. A boy on a bicycle was peddling up the hill, leaning into his handlebars with effort. No girls were in sight. Not even a dog. Bronte ate two brownies.

This was a radically dumb idea! At four o'clock she returned the plates and cups to the kitchen, then put the remaining brownies—she had now eaten four—into a freezer bag to keep herself from finishing them.

As she headed to the strand to rip down the flyers, she ran into Mom and Dad coming home early.

"Several parents came by the café to ask about the club," said her father. "They wanted to make sure we're not ax murderers or something. How did the first meeting go, honey?"

"I've changed my mind about the club," Bronte said. But then she remembered bragging about her new and improved self, her courageous heart.

"What I mean is, I'm going to start everything next week."

For the next six days, Bronte walked on the beach and explored town. There were T-shirt and souvenir shops, video and music stores, ice-cream and hot-dog stands, the deli and a bakery with the best sugar cookies she had ever tasted.

At Bikini Genie, Bronte stood outside staring at the window display. The tanned mannequins were skinny with long legs and substantial bosoms. One of the suits was like the oldies song: "Itsy Bitsy Teeny Weeny Yellow Polka Dot Bikini."

I'll never fit into one of those things. Bronte looked down at her sunburned knees and arms. She took another cookie from the white bakery bag and sighed, "I am out of style in the most cumbersome way."

* * *

Wednesday morning—book club day—Bronte showered and got dressed. She walked to town as fast as she could, along the strand, out onto the pier, and back up the hill. This kept her occupied for two hours and twenty minutes. Once again she swept the house, then set out juice and brownies— a new batch because she had eaten the others after all, straight out of the freezer.

She looked at the kitchen clock. Five minutes to three. While turning down the classical radio station, she heard a knock on the door.

Bronte held her breath. ". . . Uh . . . coming!" She hurried to the entryway.

The girl called Willow stood on the front step, holding a sack of popcorn. "Hi there," said Willow. "Hey! I remember you from the deli. So you're the book club girl? Cool. Here, I thought you might need help with some snacks." She kept talking as she walked into the house. "This place is positively darling. I used to know the people who lived here."

A moment passed before Bronte remembered her manners. "Hey, thanks for bringing popcorn. My name is Bronte. Are you—"

"Willow." She held out her hand to shake Bronte's. "Is anyone else here? I know at least seven girls who said they would come. Actually eight."

"Eight?"

"Yeah, but you know how that goes."

"Eight, really?"

Willow's eyes were a beautiful blue. Her blond hair fell below her shoulders, combed back from her face with a glittery headband that made her look chic. Bronte tugged her T-shirt down over her rear end, then led her guest to the sunroom.

"Here's where we'll meet. So far it's just us two, and—"

"Oh, how cute are *these!*" Willow said. "Crackers shaped like dog bones. I love it. Like those little cheese goldfish. May I?"

"Sure, but they're not—"

Willow reached into the dish and put several into her mouth before Bronte could stop her. It took a few chews before Willow realized her mistake. She grabbed a napkin and pressed it to her lips.

"You're quirky, Bronte."

"I'm really sorry. I was hoping someone would bring a dog."

"Don't worry about it. But if a girl named Jessie shows up, don't say anything to her about the dog biscuits. She's going into the seventh grade, too, but none of us like her."

Chapter 5

Just Two

Now Bronte was nervous about this girl, Jessie. She kept glancing out at the walkway while eating handfuls of popcorn. Only one hour and fifty-five minutes left. She hoped others would show up to help with the conversation.

"So," Bronte began, pouring Willow a glass of juice. "How long have you lived in Gray's Beach?"

"All my life. My parents moved here from Hollywood before I was born. . . ."

Fortunately for Bronte, Willow loved to talk.

At three-thirty the doorbell interrupted them.

Bronte dashed to the entryway. "Oh, hi!" she said to a girl who looked familiar.

"So sorry I'm late. My name is Nan."

"Come on in," said Bronte. It was the girl from the sailboat!

Nan's short, blond hair had white streaks from the sun, and her nose was peeling. She wore sneakers with no socks or laces, and cutoffs unraveling at the hem. Her T-shirt was several sizes too big with splatters of blue paint over the logo DONNY'S BOAT YARD.

"It's *really* nice to meet you," Bronte said, leading Nan into the sunroom. "We're in here—" A chirping interrupted her. It was coming from inside Willow's purse.

"Excuse me," Willow said, digging for her cell phone. "Hello? Already? *Mom.* We barely got started." She looked out the window. A black Mercedes convertible was turning into the driveway. A woman in sunglasses was at the wheel, a slender arm draped out over the door. A red string bracelet dangled from her wrist.

Willow rolled her eyes. "I've gotta go. Hey, do you two want to meet at the beach tomorrow? I always sit by the lifeguard tower at Fourth Street."

Bronte answered quickly. "Sure. What time?"

"I love the beach," said Nan.

"Sweet. Let's say noon," said Willow. "But

Bronte, you better wear lots of sunscreen. Looks like you'll burn easily—"

Chirp chirp . . . chirp chirp . . . Willow again flipped open her phone. "Okay! I'm coming." To the girls she said, "My mom has a hernia if she has to wait. So, see you tomorrow?"

"Yeah!"

"Bye."

Nan sat on the floor by the coffee table, eating a brownie. "Mmm . . . these are great! Did you add butterscotch chips? And . . . maybe marsh-mallows?"

"Yep. There's other stuff in there, too. It's my special recipe."

"Well, they're scrumptiously *perfect*." Now Nan eyed the dog biscuits and grinned. "Any customers yet?"

Bronte was tempted to tell about Willow. "Naw," she said. "No dogs today."

"Too bad. I love dogs."

"Same here."

"Hey," said Nan. "Maybe sometime you can come aboard."

"Your boat?"

"Yeah. We live there. Just my mom, dad, and me."

"That sounds awesome."

"Yeah, it's pretty cool. Have you been in Gray's Beach a long time? No offense, but you don't look like you're from around here."

"Duh." Bronte gave a weak smile. "We moved a couple weeks ago from Santa Fe. After my grandpa died my parents sold their restaurant. We had this humongous yard sale and got rid of most everything except our books."

Bronte glanced across the room. On either side of the fireplace, there were shelves loaded with novels, magazines, and reference books. Framed photos of her grandparents and her swim team were on the mantel. Another showed her camping in the mountains with her Girl Scout troop. She blinked fast to keep back a choked feeling.

"Bet you had lots of friends," Nan offered.

Bronte nodded.

"I know exactly how you feel."

At five o'clock the girls said good-bye on the porch. While Bronte was cleaning up the sunroom, she realized she had forgotten to mention reading a book together.

* * *

The next morning she made lunch to share with Willow and Nan: peanut butter sandwiches with dried cranberries instead of jelly, potato chips, and a rinsed-out milk jug full of water. She packed everything into a brown grocery sack, then returned to the problem of what to wear.

The last time she went swimming was at the state meet in Albuquerque. She had liked her Speedo, black with white panels along the sides. All the girls on her team wore them because it was their uniform.

But now, standing before the mirror, it was a different story. *I look like an orca!* She stared for ten seconds then grabbed her clothes.

"Fiddlesticks, etcetera, and so forth!" Over her suit she put on shorts and a baggy T-shirt. In the kitchen she wrote a note to her parents.

While heading down the hill with her lunch and a towel over her shoulder, Bronte enjoyed the ocean view more than ever. An oil tanker in the channel was heading for open sea, its wake a thin white trail, and Santa Cruz Island seemed anchored to the horizon.

I am sumptuously pleased we moved to Gray's Beach!

Chapter 6

Swimmer

Bronte sat on her towel. At the Fourth Street life-guard tower, there were adults in sand chairs with coolers, kids building castles with little pails and shovels, and several girls in bikinis—but no Willow or Nan.

Every few minutes Bronte glanced up the beach. She poured herself a cup of water, then ate half a sandwich. Even smeared with sunscreen, she felt herself getting burned.

More families arrived from the parking lot, hauling playpens and babies. They spread out blankets and put up parasols for shade. Nearby some boys were playing volleyball; others were skimming a Frisbee over the shallow waves.

It was now one o'clock. Bronte looked up the beach again.

Maybe Willow and Nan are flakes, she thought. *Maybe everyone in California is a flake. That's what my friends back home say, anyway.*

It was hot sitting in the sun in her clothes, waiting, waiting. Two girls in thongs with wobbly bottoms strolled by. They were giggling and smiling up at the lifeguard.

Okay. So I look like Shamu. Big deal. I'm a beach girl now, and friend or no friend I'm gonna swim in the ocean—today! She peeled off her T-shirt and shorts, then ran down to the shallow waves. The water was freezing. Gradually she waded out to her hips. She jumped with the swells, arms in the air to balance herself.

"Hey Bronte!" someone yelled. She turned to see Nan, coming toward her, knees high as she sloshed through the current. Her bathing suit was a yellow top with purple boardshorts cinched around the waist with a blue belt. She looked sturdy.

"Sorry I'm late!" said Nan. "Is Willow here?"

"Not yet."

"Bummer. Have you gone in all the way yet, Bronte?"

"It's my first time."

"You can't swim?" The girls were shouting to be heard above the surf.

"No, I mean in the ocean."

"Then watch what I do," yelled Nan. "See that wave breaking out there, coming this way? Duck under before it hits you, then go as deep as possible. If it churns you up, dig into the sand to hold on. Get ready . . . now!"

Just in time Bronte took a deep breath, bent her knees, and sank. She opened her eyes. The water was a beautiful pale green, swirling with bubbles. Her skin tingled, and she could taste salt. With an exhilarating push from the bottom, she burst to the surface. *Fantastication!*

Nan had drifted farther out, where a frothing line of surf was roaring toward shore. Roaring toward *them*. It looked rough. Bronte watched Nan dive under it, her curved arms and back disappearing beneath the foam. Immediately she did the same. The breaker thundered overhead, twisting her around with flailing legs. With her hands she managed to dig into the sand as Nan had instructed, until the rolling green swell passed.

Its power amazed her. She stretched for the surface and gulped for air, laughing from the thrill of it all. Nan was waving to her, also laughing. Then with a practiced stroke, Bronte swam toward her friend.

After an hour of wrestling the waves, the girls were cold and tired. They agreed to meet again the next day. Bronte's walk from the beach up the hill was slow because she was sunburned and drowsy.

The outdoor shower on her patio had a panoramic view of the harbor. Still wearing her bathing suit, Bronte stood under the hot water, looking out at Santa Cruz Island. Its faraway shape was giving her an idea. She turned off the squeaky faucets.

"Fantabulous!" she said aloud. "An impeccable book for our club!" She wrapped her towel around her shoulders, then traipsed through the house with wet feet.

Bronte's bedroom was littered with clothes. The shelves she had so meticulously organized were now cluttered with chunks of driftwood and stones gathered from the tide pools. There was a slight odor of dead fish from the purple shell of a sea urchin. Carefully she moved everything aside to read the spines of her books, trying to recall if she had last alphabetized them by author or by title.

"Aha! Authors. Scott O'Dell. Here he is." From the bottom shelf she pulled out *Island of the Blue Dolphins*, an old edition that had been her mother's as a little girl. Its cover was ragged along the edges and faded.

Bronte sat on the floor, not bothered by the puddle from her dripping suit nor that sand from her towel was sticking to her skin. She loved this story. It was about an Indian girl who spent eighteen years alone on San Nicholas Island.

In fourth grade Bronte's teacher had shown the class an aerial photograph of the rugged islands off California's coast. San Nicholas was the most remote with miles of ocean surrounding the small shape. Bronte had marveled at the idea of Indians canoeing between the islands and the mainland.

She pressed the book to her chest and

squeezed her eyes shut. She pictured Karana, the abandoned girl, all alone, without friends. Even though Bronte lived in a town full of people, at times it seemed as if *she* were alone on an island. She let out a huge sigh.

"I'll read this again tonight," she announced to her messy room. "It'll be *perfect* for palaver." She wasn't sure what *palaver* meant, but she had heard her grandfather use it when referring to conversation. In any event she liked the sound of it.

The new announcements Bronte posted for her club had her phone number and a few changes—refreshments would still be served, and dogs were welcome—but she added the most important detail:

Island of the Blue Dolphins by Scott O'Dell.
It's a GREAT story!
[Several copies are in the library.]
This Wednesday.
We'll palaver about Chapters 1–4.

Bronte had counted the pages, then divided by eight, the number of weeks remaining in the summer. She figured this way her club would have plenty of time to discuss the book.

At Davy Jones's Deli she put up her last flyer, then bought a triple-dip chocolate ice-cream cone. Though the sun was hot, she managed to eat the whole thing before it melted.

Chapter 7

A Curious Beginning

Finally it was book club day, and the girls would actually have something to discuss.

Bronte got up early and baked gingerbread while straightening the house. She washed a basket of strawberries. Knowing Nan would be coming made her feel less nervous, but still she decided a swim before lunch would be a pleasant distraction.

As she was walking downhill to the beach, a black convertible turned onto Harbor Street a block away. Bronte couldn't take her eyes off the car. Willow was in the backseat! But the startling sight was a passenger whose head was swathed in bandages like a mummy.

The scene reminded her of when Aunt Connie

had stumbled through a plate-glass door. The emergency-room doctor had put twenty stitches in her face, then wrapped her head in layers of white gauze.

So that's why Willow didn't show up the other day. A family emergency. Bronte felt guilty for assuming the girl was a flake and was glad she hadn't complained to Nan.

I'm getting good at keeping my mouth shut! Another new improvement for Bronte Bella, not gossiping. Her last month in New Mexico had been disastrous, when Bronte's friends had turned against her because she blabbed a secret. With a loud sigh, Bronte hurried through the hot sand down to the lifeguard tower. She spread out her towel, then ran into the surf.

At three o'clock that afternoon, Willow and a Hispanic girl walked up the path to Bronte's cottage. The door was open for the breeze. "Hi," she called out to them.

Willow introduced Lupe, who had long dark hair and brown eyes. "We've been best friends since kindergarten."

Lupe waved a manicured hand. She was wearing

capris with sequined sandals and a lace camisole. A red-feathered boa was wrapped around her neck. She gave it a twirl, then pointed a dainty foot as if ready to dance.

"Wow," Bronte said. "You two have known each other a long time." She avoided looking at her own feet, at her horrible huaraches. Her flip-flops were still on the patio, sandy from the beach. "I have friends, too, from kindergarten, but they live in—"

"This is such a cute house. I *love* it." Lupe pivoted in front of the hall mirror, looking at herself sideways, chin held high. She smiled at Bronte's reflection. "Oh, I'm sorry. Where did you say your friends live?"

"New Mexico—"

"Willow and I still know a boy from when we were five years old. He's a big-name surfer now with an endorsement. He was in a commercial for Quicksilver."

"Oh." Bronte's voice was lost in the chatter as Willow and Lupe settled in the sunroom. A few minutes later Nan walked in the open door.

Bronte said, "I am *so* glad you're here." She made introductions, then started passing around the refreshments. This time Bronte had left the dog bones in the kitchen, to avoid any misunderstanding.

Everyone wrote phone numbers and e-mail addresses on Bronte's notepad; then there was an awkward silence as she tried to think of how to start the meeting. She knew it was unlikely, but she wished Willow would explain the mummy from a few hours earlier. Now *that* would make an interesting icebreaker.

"Okay," Bronte began, "did anyone have a chance to get through the first four chapters? I know the title was late notice but—"

"Well, it's about time you showed up, Jessie," said Willow.

All eyes turned to the brunette who had come into the room. Bronte stood up to welcome her, but the new girl was glaring at Willow. They could be twins except for their different hair color.

"You told me the meeting had been changed to three-thirty, Willow," said the girl, "so I'm not late. You're just compulsively early like always. I swear." Jessie then slumped into one of the bamboo chairs by the window and stared out at the ocean. Her jaw was tight.

Silence filled the room.

Bronte jumped up and closed the door. No one was saying anything. She filled a plate with two strawberries and some gingerbread.

"Here you go, Jessie," Bronte said, handing her the snacks. "We hadn't really started, so you're not late."

The girl didn't respond.

Chapter 8

An Empty Chair

Nan broke the silence.

"My parents and I sailed to San Nicholas Island last summer," she said. "To celebrate my eleventh birthday."

"That's so cool," was Bronte's quick response. She did not want the conversation to lag. "Did you camp there? I've heard people can camp on some of the Channel Islands."

"No. It's a military base now. Sometimes they allow scuba divers, but we had to anchor a hundred yards offshore for the night. It took all day to sail there from Catalina. That's where I grew up."

Jessie let out a sigh of exasperation. "So you're an island girl. And your point is?"

Nan shrugged. "I don't know. I just thought it

was interesting that I've seen where Karana had lived for so long. There really are dolphins and—"

"Who's Karana?" asked Jessie.

Willow broke in. *"Hello?* The main character in the novel you obviously haven't started reading, *Jessie."*

"Well, who made *you* boss? At least I don't cheat."

"Cheat?"

"Yeah. Watching the movie instead of reading a book is cheating. I sat next to you in English last year, remember?"

"Well, Jessie, at least I don't ignore people when they try to be friendly."

Nan and Lupe exchanged glances, then looked over at Bronte who turned her palms up. This wasn't what she expected.

"Island of the Blue Dolphins is a really good story," Bronte said softy. "I haven't seen the movie, but it's no big deal if someone doesn't read it. Really."

"Then why are we even here?" Jessie asked.

Bronte froze. She was starting to wonder that herself.

Then came Nan's voice. "I was in a book club on Catalina, about six of us. The librarian was in charge, but it was still a lot of fun. And it's a way to get to know people." She reached for her glass of juice, setting it on her knee. "I'm new in town; we sailed here a few weeks ago. So far I've talked to a lifeguard and a surfer, but you're the first girls I've met."

There was a clatter of plates as Bronte started passing around the gingerbread and strawberries, then pouring more juice, something to fill the silence that now hung in the room.

"What was it like living on an island?" Bronte asked. "I grew up in the desert. It's way different there."

Nan laughed, then began talking. She was animated, motioning with her hands to describe a seven-legged octopus she once found in a tide pool. Bronte glanced at the other girls. They appeared to be listening, but they also were studying Nan's ragged cutoffs and oversized T-shirt.

". . . and it was super windy at San Nicholas Island, like in the book. Remember where Karana talked about blowing sand, how it stung her skin?"

"Yeah," Lupe said. "I loved how she described everything."

"Me too," said Willow. "It seemed so beautiful. The Indians could swim whenever they wanted."

"You know," said Lupe, sitting up straight, shoulders back. "If they ever make another movie, I'm going to audition for the lead. I'm at least a twelfth-generation Californian. My dad says our ancestors lived on these islands. He insists I go to college, but I want to be an actress."

"Lupe, you would be great in films," Willow said.

"I know," she agreed.

As the conversation relaxed, so did Bronte. She excused herself to get more napkins from the kitchen and to peek at the clock.

Whew, just one more hour to go.

When Bronte returned from the kitchen, the girls were looking at the front door, which now stood wide open. The breeze caught the napkins in her hand, fluttering them to the floor. They were from Popeye's Deli. As she bent to gather them up, she noticed the chair by the window was empty.

"Did Jessie leave?" she asked. "What happened?"

Lupe looked confused. "We were discussing how the Aleuts murdered Karana's father, and I said I would hate for anyone in my family to die, you know, or to disappear. That's all I said."

Bronte lowered herself into the empty chair and gazed out the window.

A veritable disaster. She remembered her grandfather saying this last summer when he crashed his golf cart into the lake. Things today had been going fine until Jessie got upset and left, which wasn't quite a disaster. But to Bronte it felt close. Veritably close.

Chapter 9

Surfer Girls

The Boogie board was wrapped with a bow, propped against a wall in the breakfast nook. When Bronte came into the kitchen, she could smell cinnamon toast and freshly brewed coffee.

"Surprise!" said her father.

"Happy Half Birthday," said Mom.

"Oh, wow, thank you!" Bronte picked the board up. It stood as tall as her shoulders and was as light as Styrofoam. It fit easily under her arm for carrying. "This is perfect. Nan and I are meeting by the pier today so now we'll each have one. I can't wait. It's gonna be a blast. Thanks again." Bronte hugged her mom then kissed her dad's clean-shaven cheek. She loved the aroma of his Old Spice cologne.

*   *   *

It was sunny, and the beach was crowded. Waves at the pier were dotted with kids on canvas surf mats and Boogie boards, most riding in on their bellies, some trying to stand like surfers.

Bronte Velcroed the leash to the board around her ankle after watching how Nan did it. As they headed for the water, a woman in a bikini walked by.

"Those things are hideous, especially thongs," Nan said as they paddled out for their first wave. "They're uncomfortable, plus the bottoms always slip off in the surf. Trust me."

Bronte smiled. Her Shamu one-piece felt better all ready.

Despite the bright sunshine the water was cold. After an hour they were shivering, but by then Bronte had learned which swells to catch: the good ones that pushed her over the crest of a wave, dropping her down into the foam for an exhilarating ride to shore.

"Yeee!" she and Nan screamed with each free fall; then as their boards scraped against the wet beach, they jumped up to swim out again.

*   *   *

"So do you think Jessie'll come back for more *palaver*?" Nan asked when they got out of the water. "That's a *delectable* word. I've been using it all week to my parents' *consternation*." She laughed, then stretched out in the hot sand, not using her towel. "I love words, don't you?"

"More than chocolate," said Bronte, still standing up. She was freezing. "Hey, doesn't it bug you to lie in the sand with it all sticking to your skin?"

"Nope. You get warm faster, and it'll brush off. Try it, Bronte. So what's your favorite word?"

"Oh, definitely *perambulator*."

"Meaning?"

"It's a baby buggy with big wheels, like British nannies use." Bronte lowered herself to her stomach, scooping a pillow of sand for her chin as Nan had done. The warmth reminded her of the hot springs after swimming in a mountain stream. She felt drowsy. It would be easy to fall asleep.

"Nan? You awake?"

"Mmm-hmm."

"To answer your other question, I hope that Jessie comes back."

"Me too."

"So what d'you think's going on with her?" Bronte asked. "Why'd she get so upset?"

"Don't know." Nan leaned on her elbow to look at Bronte. "What I can't figure out is why she and Willow are so mean to each other. And Willow is *mendacious*. I like that word, don't you?"

"Very much. But why did Willow lie about what time the club started? Anyway, I've got Jessie's phone number. Think I should give her a call?"

"What for?"

"To see how she's doing. Invite her to the beach with us, etcetera."

"Betcha she won't come."

"Why do you say that?"

"Bronte, didn't you notice how pale she is? I mean, *really* pale, more than you, like she's been sitting inside forever, and she's a brunette. They don't burn like you redheads."

"Well, maybe Jessie just needs someone to invite her." Bronte remembered her first day in Gray's Beach when *she* was afraid to go out of the house.

While she pondered this, a drama was unfolding under a nearby parasol. From where Bronte lay with her cheek in the sand, she could see a pack of seagulls waddling by a picnic basket that had been left unattended. One of them pecked at part of sandwich, while another managed to steal it from him and take flight.

Sudden squawks of complaint filled the air along with cries from other gulls now swooping overhead in chase. Bronte rolled onto her back and shaded her eyes to watch. In the end the sandwich fell to the ground where a waiting bird snatched and swallowed it.

The squabbling seagulls brought to mind something her dad often said about people who were unhappy with one another: *Every story has two sides, Bronte. There's usually a darned good reason why someone is upset.*

Chapter 10

Out of Control

After another swim, Nan and Bronte agreed to meet again the following day. Bronte carried her Boogie board home under her arm with her towel around her neck, as she had seen the locals do.

In the kitchen, she ate a cookie while dialing Jessie's number. On the third ring a woman answered.

"Hello?"

"Hi. This is Bronte Bella. May I please speak to Jessie?"

A muffled moment passed. "Oh! Is this about the book club?"

"Yes."

"Hold on. I'll get her."

Bronte could hear voices in the background.

She couldn't tell, but they sounded angry. Soon she realized Jessie and her mother were arguing about the club.

"It's lame, that's why. I'm not going, and you can't make me."

"You listen to me, young lady—"

Should I hang up? It felt as if she were eavesdropping.

"—people will think you're smart, Jessie, if you know how to discuss literature. It's quite the thing to do, even your brother—"

"I'm not an idiot, you know."

"Well, my dear, that's a debate worth having."

Bronte hung up.

At the next meeting Lupe arrived wearing sunglasses in leopard-print frames with a matching scarf swirled over her shoulders. She handed Bronte a small cardboard box from the bakery. Inside were oatmeal cookies and date bars. "My dad's the owner," she said, "so he loves giving stuff to my friends."

"Wow, thanks, Lupe. I'll get a plate." Bronte hurried into the kitchen, optimistic that this time would be more cheerful than the last. She set the cookies on the coffee table just as Nan showed up, soon followed by Willow.

When Jessie came in she went to the bamboo chair without greeting anyone. After the unpleasant episode last time, Bronte was surprised she was back, and glad. But feeling awkward about the aborted phone call, she glanced down at her notes.

"Sooo," she began, "I was wondering what you guys thought about Chapter Five, where Karana's people wanted to canoe to Catalina Island. It's about fifty miles away, and the channel is real choppy. See, this map here—"

"I went to camp on Catalina," Willow volunteered. "Girl Scouts. We slept on the beach, but the wild boars came down from the hills and stole our toothbrushes that we left out."

"Okay . . . well . . ." Bronte didn't want to cut her off, but she knew Willow could talk forever, and they should at least *try* to discuss the book. At their last meeting, after Jessie left, the girls had ended up reading Lupe's *People* magazine together, then gossiping about boys in town.

"Anyway," continued Willow, "me and my friends shaved our legs there for the first time ever. The camp store had bars of cocoa butter for sale so we used—"

"Me too!" Now it was Lupe. "I mean, I first started shaving at camp. My mom went ballistic because she didn't get to show me how. Like I really want to do things the way *she* does. Anyway"—Lupe adjusted her scarf—"we made up. Now she buys me Sweet Teen Shaving Gel with pink razors, and makes a fuss about me growing up." Lupe rolled her eyes dramatically.

"My mom doesn't shave her legs," Nan volunteered. "She doesn't even wear a bra."

"Oh you wouldn't believe *my* mother," said Willow. "She has every color, and they're all padded to make her boobs bigger. She gave me a training bra when I turned nine, even though—"

"Okay," Bronte interrupted, uneasy with such intimate details. She wanted to steer the conversation back to their book but didn't know how. As a result the next hour and a half roared by with Nan, Willow, and Lupe chattering about cell phones, celebrities, pets, and finally parents. They didn't seem to notice that Bronte and Jessie were silent.

Bronte felt helpless. She was thrilled that

everyone was getting along, but the meeting was out of control, and it was nearly five o'clock. Making one last effort she held up her copy of *Island of the Blue Dolphins*. "Since we're on the subject of parents, this was my mom's when she was ten years—"

"My mom hates me." It was the first time Jessie had spoken that afternoon. She was staring down at her sandals, fiddling with a silver chain around her ankle.

Willow drew in a breath, ready to comment; but Bronte headed her off.

"Jessie," Bronte said, "I'm sure your mother doesn't hate you. Even when we're awful our mothers love us, right?" Bronte looked at the others for confirmation, but no one responded.

"Yeah. Right." Jessie stood up. "This club is stupid." She slung her handbag over her shoulder and left the sunroom.

When the front door slammed shut, Bronte dropped her head back and stared at the ceiling fan.

Now what?

Chapter 11

New Neighbor

The next day, Bronte and Nan met on the pier. They looked out at the bay where Nan's sailboat was moored.

Bronte was trying to picture how they would get out *there* from *here*.

The sloop Nan lived on with her parents was forty-eight feet long with all the signs of a family. A potted geranium was on deck, roped to the single mast; colorful beach towels were hanging over the boom; and flying from the jib were some sheets and pillowcases drying in the sun.

"We're waiting for a slip to become available at the docks," Nan said. "It's a hassle rowing in to the little yacht club for our showers and e-mail.

If the water's choppy, it makes me late for everything. Anyway, for now we're commuters. Ready?" She laughed in a cheerful way that made Bronte smile.

Nan bent under a railing where there was a ladder attached to one of the pilings. She started down. "Come on, Bronte, it's not as bad as it looks."

Bronte looked at the water far below. Tied to the ladder was a rubber dinghy. It bobbed in the swell like a small toy. "But we're so high up!" she cried. "What if we fall?"

"It's all right," Nan called up to her. "I do this every day. It's the quickest way to reach the boat. It would take an hour to row from the docks."

"I don't know about this." Bronte held tight to each rung, clinging tighter the farther down she went. Waves sloshed against the piling. Moss beneath her feet felt gooshy, and when one of her flip-flops slipped off, her heart jumped. She watched over her shoulder as it fell, wobbling in the wind like a Frisbee.

Nan reached into the water for it, but it floated away. "Sorry!" she yelled. "Just a few more steps, and you're here." Her voice echoed from the underbelly of the pier.

Bronte lowered herself past dark clusters of barnacles attached to the piling. Eventually she felt a hand on her ankle, steadying her into the dinghy. She landed in a sprawl, glad for the rounded sides.

"You made it!" Nan untied the rope—she called it a painter—then took up the oars. "We'll be there in a couple minutes." With strong arms she rowed through the bumpy water, spray splashing over the bow. Bronte was amazed at how easily Nan maneuvered them alongside the *Avalon Rose*. But as they rounded the port side, a stink of dead fish hit them.

"Eeeew," they cried as they came upon the odor. A shiny brown seal was sunning himself on the swimming platform that extended below the stern.

"Shoo!" Nan yelled. She rattled the oarlocks, but he merely regarded her with drowsy eyes. "He comes here every morning, sometimes with one of his buddies. We let him lie here until we can't stand the smell." More rattling . . . then he slid into the water and swam away.

Nan tied the painter to a cleat by the platform. Then in one graceful step, she climbed up into the stern and extended a hand to Bronte.

"Welcome aboard," she said. "It's our home sweet home."

Chapter 12

Fins in the Water

Bronte and Nan were belowdecks, in a long, narrow cabin. The walls were paneled in teak with racks of books in corners and under the portholes. Shelves had bungee cords to keep things from falling. Everything looked compact and tidy, especially the galley with its miniature stove and oven, an ice chest instead of a refrigerator, cupboards, and a sink small enough for a playhouse.

Nan pointed out the ship-to-shore radio and navigation system. "My parents work on boats in dry dock sanding and painting the hulls, so we're not rich. They try to live as simply as possible," she said. "You know, go to the library and secondhand stores. It's the three Rs: recycle, reduce, reuse. I'm not miserable, but I do wish we had TV."

"Same here," said Bronte. "Sometimes it's too quiet at our house."

"Join the club."

As Bronte surveyed the cabin, she noticed that nothing matched. Some of the bench cushions around the table were brown, others blue-striped. The curtains on either side of the portholes had been sewn from faded beach towels. Dishcloths drying over the sink were ragged, but clean. Nan's bunk was under the quarterdeck. Her bed was covered with a patchwork quilt made from T-shirts with sailboat names.

Bronte felt right at home. Another family as weird as hers. "I like it here," she said.

"Thanks. So do I, most of the time. Hey, wanna go for a swim?"

"Here? Off the boat?"

"Yeah, it's a blast."

"Uh . . . okay. I guess."

Nan tossed a pair of boardshorts to her, then a tank top. She opened the door of what appeared to be a small closet. "You can change in here. Sailors call it the head."

Bronte stepped over a six-inch threshold into the tiniest bathroom she had ever seen. The sink was the size of a cereal bowl and there was no shower or tub. Rolled up towels and magazines were in cubbyholes. She stood on her tiptoes to look out an opened skylight just as a pelican swooped low over the water. She changed quickly, several times bumping her elbows against the walls.

Nan met her on deck with a pair of fins. "Have you ever used one of these?" she asked.

"Swim team," Bronte answered. "When I was learning the butterfly kick."

"Then you'll love it in the ocean. With the salt water it feels like you're floating."

They boosted themselves over the stern, then sat on the sunny platform where the seal had been napping. It was level with the water. They each put on one flipper, then slid in.

"Yikes!" Bronte shrieked. It was colder than in the surf and way, *way* over her head. The water was so clear she could see thirty feet to the bottom where stalks of kelp were anchored in the sand. It was like looking down upon a forest of brown lace waving in the current. Tiny fish darted among shafts of sunlight.

The girls swam around the *Avalon Rose*, daring

each other to touch the slimy anchor chain, then the slimy buoy. Most of the boats moored in the harbor had dinghies or little outboards rafted alongside.

"We have to be careful swimming out here," Nan said, "because basically no one can see us. A propeller would chop us—"

"Aaggh!" Bronte screamed, suddenly splashing her arms and legs. "Nan! Something bumped me!"

Nan stretched her neck to look around. "What? What?"

"*Underwater.* It felt rubbery. It was big." Bronte was beginning to panic, her breath coming in gasps.

"It's probably a seal. They're all over—"

"I don't care. Let's get out of here."

"Okay, but try not to freak out, Bronte."

"I can't help it. Let's hurry."

As Bronte swam for the boat, she saw something out the corner of her eye and stopped to tread water. "Nan? What's that over there?"

Near an orange buoy twenty feet away, a dark fin was slicing the surface. Then there were three fins, circling.

Chapter 13

Blue, Not Gray

Bronte felt sick with dread.

She was doomed. Her parents would have to identify her mangled body at the morgue, if there was even anything left of it. A million thoughts raced through her mind the way they do before you die, or so she had read. Her throat felt lumpy.

"Nan." It came out as a whisper. "Nan, what d'we do?"

"Not sure." Nan was choking from gulped salt water. She coughed. "Whatever you do, don't splash. The sharks will think we're prey and come after us for sure."

"Great." Bronte watched the fins. There were five now. They seemed to be coming closer, but it was hard to tell from so low in the water. She wished they were still up in the boat.

Well, at least I'll die with a friend. Bronte felt her muscles tense as she shivered with cold and with fear. Though she was an excellent swimmer, it was getting hard to keep afloat.

"Bronte?"

"Yeah?"

"Bronte, look. Over there."

The fins were coming fast. But just then, one of them curved out of the water in a graceful leap.

"Dolphins!" yelled Nan. "They're just dolphins. Thank God. Bronte, see how they're blue, not gray like a shark?"

"I've never *seen* a shark! How should *I* know!"

Bronte was too unnerved to appreciate that they were swimming with dolphins, and they weren't even in a theme park. One of them glided nearby, its large eye looking at her, curious. It was at least six feet long. It didn't touch her, but Bronte could feel a warm current underwater as it passed inches away. Her heart pounded in her chest. These were *big* animals.

Not until she and Nan were safely on deck

with towels around their shoulders, did Bronte begin to relax. She breathed in the salt air. She listened to the seagulls. What came to mind were the pages she'd reread last night.

"Hey, Nan. Have you read Chapter Ten yet, where Karana paddles away from San Nicholas Island?"

"Yeah! I love that part; when her canoe starts leaking, and she has to turn back. Then the dolphins escort her till she's safe. They've done that with this boat, Bronte, when we've been out in the channel. They leap around both sides of our bow while we're sailing for shore. It's so cool."

"You're kidding. They really do that?"

"Yep."

"Wow." Bronte thought for a moment. "You know how Karana thinks the dolphins are a good omen? How they make her happy because she's not alone? Maybe they're a good omen for us, too, Nan."

"I bet they are. Let's just say they are."

"Now I wish I'd petted the one that swam by me. He looked friendly, actually."

"Bronte, you were too freaked out."

"Yeah."

"You know what else is cool?" Nan said. "When we were out at San Nicholas Island, Dad and I went snorkeling. Two of them swam so close all I had to do was reach out my hand. It was lovely in the most *astonishing* way. Their skin feels like our rubber dinghy! And it looks like they're smiling at you."

"Oh, Nan," Bronte burst out. She hugged her then she quickly sat back down. "Thank you for taking me swimming. We got to be with the dolphins together. Like Karana."

The *Avalon Rose* rocked gently in the swells. Looking toward the beach, all Bronte and Nan could see were the roofs of lifeguard towers and the backside of waves as they rolled into shore. They could hear the distant, happy shrieks of kids on Boogie boards.

"I forgot to ask if you ever called Jessie," Nan said.

"Uh . . . yeah."

"Well, what d'she say?"

Bronte was remembering the harsh words between Jessie and her mother. Boy, was she tempted to spill those juicy details.

"Well, I did call," she replied, "but I didn't get through to her." There. It wasn't a lie. It was the new and improved Bronte Bella, trying not to gossip.

Nan went belowdecks, then returned with a box of Cheez-Its and cups of water, which she set on the cushion between them. "I've got an idea, Bronte."

"What?"

"Well, what if we have one of our meetings here, on the boat? I already asked my mom and dad, and they said it's okay. We can palaver right *here*."

"Hmm." Bronte squinted toward the pier, wishing she had worn sunglasses against the glare.

"If you're thinking about the dinghy, don't worry," said Nan. "Mine holds five easy, or we can use my parents'. Theirs is bigger with two sets of oars. It won't be a problem."

"Actually, I was thinking about something else."

"You mean Jessie?"

"Yeah. What if we're all out here, surrounded by water, and Jessie gets upset again?"

"Well, she won't be able to run away. She acts like she hates us, but I don't think she does."

A sudden splashing came from the stern, then a fetid odor. A seal slid onto the diving platform and gave the girls a serious look. His wet whiskers were silvery in the sunlight.

"Your buddy's back," Bronte said.

"Hello, butterball," Nan called. She tossed him some crackers, which floated by his flipper. Rolling into the water, he slurped them up.

Bronte laughed. "It's so cool out here, Nan. Maybe Jessie will like it, too."

Chapter 14

A Day of Surprises

The following Wednesday, Bronte went to the deli for lunch. It was crowded so she took the last empty stool at the counter. She noticed Willow at the table behind her, but a row of tall, potted ferns separated them. Willow was talking to the waitress, Dorothy.

". . . So your guidance counselor is arranging a tutor. That's great."

"Yeah, but not till school starts," Willow said. "For now she wants me to keep practicing. Said the book club is a good idea, but I'm not sure."

"Why's that, honey?"

"Well, I get nervous. What if they start reading out loud, Miss Dorothy? What if the girls find out that—" A clatter of dishes drowned out Willow's voice.

Bronte ate her cheeseburger slowly. *What are they talking about?* She strained to hear more, but the lunch hour noise only grew louder. When she finished her coleslaw and pickle, she left a dollar tip on the counter, then went to the cashier. Willow was already there, paying for her salad.

"Hey, Quirky Girl," said Willow. "Didn't know you were in here, too. Sure is crowded today."

"Yeah." Bronte shoved her hands in her pockets. "Oh, hey. Book club's this afternoon. At my house again. Think you'll be able to come?"

"Uh . . . maybe. I don't know. My mother made an appointment with a photographer, for my portfolio. When she lived in Hollywood, she used to do commercials and thinks I should, too. *Whatever.* Anyway . . . uh, when we're done, maybe she can drop me off at your house. Well, I gotta go."

Willow waved good-bye then hurried out into the sunshine. She was wearing a short skirt with a sash and halter top that hugged her ribs. Her belly was tan and trim.

She could be in a Coppertone commercial, Bronte thought, watching the girl head home along the beach. *But what's she trying to hide?*

Bronte planned the meeting for out back on the brick patio, under the shade of a eucalyptus tree. While she swept the bricks, she kept wondering why Willow was nervous about the book club.

Soon all the girls arrived, including Willow, and also an interesting visitor. They seated themselves in low beach chairs and began passing around the snacks Nan had brought: grapes and granola bars.

"Hi guys," Bronte said. "First I want to welcome Lupe's friend, Sonny Boy. He's eight months old."

The girls reached out to pet the golden retriever sitting at attention beside Lupe. He wore a blue scarf around his neck that matched Lupe's. Ears alert, he appeared to be smiling, and his wagging tail made him shiver. Sonny Boy seemed ready to explode with curiosity. When he noticed a doggie treat move from Bronte's pocket to her hand, he could no longer contain himself.

With one big puppy pounce, he knocked

Bronte over in her chair and upturned the snack table. She choked with laughter. *I knew a dog would cheer things up!* His paws held her down while he sniffed out her pocket, which now spilled forth a dozen tiny biscuits.

"I am *so* embarrassed," Lupe said. She helped Bronte—who was still laughing—straighten her chair. Willow turned on the garden hose to refill the pitcher and passed around clean paper cups. Nan rescued the grapes that hadn't been stepped on. Jessie gathered the flying napkins.

Bronte began. "So, I've been cogitating. What would any of us do if we saw our families—like what happened to Karana—sail away from the island, leaving us all alone? I would be mortified and flabbergasted."

Lupe responded first. With her hand outstretched she gazed into the distance as if addressing an audience. "I would stomp around and weep, then swoon. I would grieve deeply and pray a lot, perhaps sing a few hymns, then start all over again. Definitely I would die a miserable, brokenhearted death, famished and forlorn."

"Ditto," said Willow.

Nan looked out at the ocean. "I wonder why Karana didn't give up. San Nicholas Island is so windy and so lonely. If this wasn't based on a true story, I would never believe it."

"Me neither," said Bronte.

Suddenly it was five o'clock. The girls looked at one another, surprised it was time to go. The black Mercedes was just pulling in the driveway, honking, as Willow's cell phone began ringing from inside her purse. She twisted around in her chair to glare out at her mother. Meanwhile Lupe clipped a leash to Sonny Boy's collar, then waved good-bye, a handsome duo in their matching scarves. Nan helped empty the trash. Jessie found the broom behind the kitchen door and swept the patio.

That night Bronte lay in bed listening to the ocean. She watched her curtain move in the breeze and smiled. The book club had not been a disaster. Willow had come after all. A dog had finally showed up, and nobody had argued. Jessie hadn't said one word the entire time, but she hadn't run away, either.

Bronte had even heard her laughing.

Chapter 15

Low Tide

At dawn the next day the sky was gray with fog. Bronte waited on the pier until Nan rowed through the mist and climbed up the ladder.

"Ready?"

"Ready!"

They made their way to the beach then hiked along the shore to Lighthouse Point. The air was still, except for the distant clang of buoys and the hum of a foghorn. Surfers in wet suits sat on their boards, waiting for a wave.

At the tide pools Nan and Bronte leaped among rocks that were pockmarked from eons of swirling water. Each pool was its own aquarium, alive with starfish of different colors and sizes;

spiky sea urchins; red crabs and brown ones; and anemones, pink with feathery heads.

"Look!" the girls kept calling to each other. Bronte crouched to watch a giant sea slug the size of a shoe box, repulsive but beautiful under the rippled water. It quivered like jelly when she touched it.

The narrow beach was littered with driftwood, from odd planks of wood to logs and branches worn smooth from rolling in the surf. To Bronte it appeared as if there had been a shipwreck. She inspected a soggy boat cushion, a long length of yellow rope, and a plastic baby bottle. When a small wave washed over her feet, she looked up.

"Tide's coming in!" she called to Nan, who had been equally absorbed.

They climbed the breakwater to watch the surfers, sitting on the driest rock they could find. They recognized some of the lifeguards paddling over the glassy swells.

Bronte liked having a friend she could be quiet with. After some minutes Nan took two apples from her day pack and handed one to her.

"So the book club seems to be coming along," Nan said.

"Yeah." Bronte took her time eating her apple. "Except . . . Nan, the other day I heard something peculiar. You'll never guess."

"What?"

"Willow's freaking out about the club."

"Really? Why?"

"She's worried we'll make her read out loud."

"That's weird."

"I know," Bronte said.

The girls looked out at the waves.

"Well, maybe she stutters," Nan suggested. "I mean, Willow loves to talk, but maybe when she reads in front of people she gets tongue-tied. Or what if she just plain can't read very well? You saw how mad she got when Jessie accused her of watching movies instead of reading in their English class."

"But why would she join a book club—" Bronte stopped herself. She had managed not to gossip about Jessie or about the mummy in Willow's car, so why was she blabbing now?

Bronte, her parents had told her a jillion times,

if you can't say anything nice about someone, don't say anything at all.

"Nan," she quickly said, "we should keep this to ourselves."

"Okay."

Chapter 16

Unintended Trouble

After sitting on the breakwater for an hour, Nan and Bronte relocated to the beach, making camp by the lifeguard tower. Bronte had managed not to talk about Willow during this time, but suddenly she couldn't help herself.

"I still don't get it," Bronte said. "Why would Willow join a book club if she has trouble reading? Maybe she's just desperate for friends—"

"Hi guys." It was Lupe. As planned she was joining them for the afternoon. She wore a see-through shift over her bathing suit and a sassy straw hat. Her brown hair was loose down her back. Today her sunglasses had turquoise rims, to match her sandals.

Settling onto her towel she said, "What were you saying about Willow?"

Nan and Bronte looked at each other.

"Did you say she can't read?" Lupe asked. "That she's desperate for friends?"

"Not exactly," said Bronte.

"Well, what then?"

Nan rolled over on her towel to face Lupe. "Willow's freaking out about the book club."

"What do you mean, she's freaking out?"

"Willow has a reading problem," Nan declared. "She's afraid we're going to make her read out loud."

"Where'd you hear this?"

"Bronte told me."

Lupe lowered her sunglasses to glare at Bronte. "You're not even from around here. Willow has been my best friend my whole life, so if she had trouble reading I think she would have told me."

Bronte was getting a headache. She shielded her eyes from the sun with a shaky hand. "Lupe, I probably misunderstood—"

"Willow's going to be so totally ticked at you," Lupe said. "You're making all this up because she's going to be a Hollywood star and you're just—"

"I'm sorry, Lupe."

"—you're just jealous."

"I never should've said anything. Please don't tell Willow."

Lupe turned her back on the girls. She reached into her straw bag and flipped open her cell phone.

"No, please don't," Bronte said.

But it was too late. Lupe had hit automatic dial and was already reporting what she had just heard.

Chapter 17

At Suds 'n' Duds

The phone in the kitchen rang. Bronte looked up from *Wuthering Heights*, the book she was reading in her bedroom. She could hear her mother set a pot on the stove, then answer.

"Bronte," she called. "For you. It's Willow."

Bronte felt her mouth go dry. She made her way slowly down the hallway, through the dining room, into the kitchen.

"Hello?"

"I thought you were my friend."

Bronte took the phone around the corner so her mother couldn't hear. "Willow?" She didn't know what else to say.

"Why are you saying bad things about me?

You're just like Jessie, the super snob. I thought you were different, Bronte."

"I didn't—"

Click.

Bronte gently replaced the phone on the hook.

After dinner it was still light outside. Barefoot, Bronte rode her bike to the Laundromat where there was a phone booth. Since her parents wouldn't let her have a cell phone until she turned thirteen, it was the only way to have a private conversation.

She locked her bike to a rack. From her pocket she pulled out a crumpled scrap of paper, put a quarter into the phone slot, then tapped in Willow's number.

Voice mail answered.

"Willow, it's Bronte," she said to the recording. "Could we please meet? I'm at Suds 'n' Duds. It's six-thirty. If you get this message, I'll be here until eight. Please come if you can. Thanks. Bye."

Bronte tried not to look like she was waiting for someone so she sat on a curb that overlooked the bay. The crowds were gone; the parking lots, empty. A few swimmers were in front of the life-guard tower. Surfers were farther away, by the pier.

"So what do you want?" A voice startled Bronte.

"Willow! Thanks so much for coming." Bronte jumped up, brushing sand from her cutoffs. She had practiced her apology, but suddenly her mind went blank. "Uh . . ."

"I don't have all night, you know."

"I . . . okay . . . Willow, can I buy you an ice-cream cone?"

"*Ice cream?* Are you crazy? What do I want with ice cream? I'm on a diet."

"But you're skinny."

Willow shook her hair off her shoulder. The breeze was blowing golden wisps over her eyes. "What do you want, Bronte?" she asked again.

"I made a terrible mistake." Bronte looked away from the girl's angry face.

Willow was silent.

"It was wrong of me to talk behind your back. Willow, I'm really sorry. I heard you telling Miss Dorothy about—"

"You're new to Gray's Beach."

"Yes," said Bronte.

"So there's a lot you don't know, okay? First off, my mother doesn't want me to be like my brainiac sister who is married and chubby, never mind that she's so smart she's in her second year of med school. What really bugs Mom is that my sister looks like a housewife."

Bronte listened, grateful that Willow liked to talk.

"So," continued Willow, "Mom keeps me busy with dance lessons and acting, and modeling, dreaming I'll make it big in Hollywood. To her school has always been a waste of time. All summer she has tried to keep me away from this book club. She says that if I sit around reading, I'll get a big butt. And to my mother a big butt is practically the worst thing that can happen to a girl. I want to be like my *sister*, not shallow like my—oh, why am I even telling you all this?"

"Willow?"

"*What!*"

"I have a big butt and—".

"What . . . are . . . you . . . talking . . . about?"

"What I mean is, I'm not perfect."

"No kidding."

Bronte clenched her fists at her side. "My over-sized gluteus maximus isn't from reading books, Willow. It's from too many brownies and cookies. I am woefully undisciplined."

"Your gluteus *what*? What does that even *mean*?" Willow's eyes filled with tears. She turned away and ran toward the water.

Chapter 18

Sitting Quietly

The sun was setting behind Lighthouse Point. Bronte looked at her watch. In thirty minutes it would start getting dark. Willow was still sitting at the water's edge.

She walked down and sat beside her. The sand was wet from a receding wave, bubbling from the tiny crabs digging underneath for air. Sandpipers on their long stilted legs raced back and forth, always safely out of reach from the lapping water. The tide left behind a line of foam in the sand, like a lace hem on a brown skirt. It was all so lovely, except that Willow was crying.

Bronte took a breath. "I don't blame you if you never speak to me again. You don't have to listen, so if you get up and leave, I'll understand."

A breaking wave curled toward shore, its crest glistening in the last rays of sunlight. Bronte waited until it had crashed and swooshed. "Gray's Beach was supposed to be my new beginning," she said. "A fresh start. There's a reason I haven't talked to my friends back home since I moved here. There's a reason they don't answer my e-mails." Bronte coughed, her voice suddenly raspy.

"Willow, I'm utterly miserable about this, but here goes. Okay. Well, right before we left New Mexico, I did something really lame. Totally lame. I blabbed my best friend's secret to another friend, and *she* told *her* best friend who told the whole swim team. Everyone was so mad at me, no one came to my going-away party. I sat there alone until Mom finally took the refreshments to a neighbor. We left the next day. I never got to say good-bye."

Bronte dug her toes into the mud. "Anyway, on that dastardly hot drive across the desert, I made up my mind about a lot of things. One of them was to never gossip again. Never ever, ever."

The girls sat without speaking as the sun spread an orange glow behind the silhouette of Santa

Cruz Island. When the incoming tide rushed over their feet, splashing them, they both jumped up.

"I better get going," Bronte said. "My parents worry if I'm not in by dark."

They walked together up the beach, to the strand. Willow waited at the Laundromat while Bronte unlocked her bike, then they continued together up the hill. On the road where they were to go their separate ways, they stopped.

"So"—Bronte chewed on her lip—"so, Willow, I'm still learning how to be a friend."

Willow sighed, then turned for her street.

As Bronte rode her bike into the driveway, she thought about their odd little book club. Willow *wants* to go, but her mother hates the idea and is preparing her for a career in Hollywood. For some reason Jessie *doesn't* want to go, but *her* mother is making her. Lupe is the one who wants to be a movie star, but *her* parents insist she plan for college. Then there is Nan. Mellow and appreciative, Nan tries to see the good in everyone and everything.

When Bronte reached the front porch, Mom was just coming down the steps with a flashlight.

"Everything okay?" she asked.

"Yeah Mom, thanks. Everything's fine." It wasn't true, but Bronte knew she would burst into tears if she started explaining. She hugged her mother good night, then went inside.

While Bronte got ready for bed, she opened her window. A breeze rattled the strings of shells hanging from a trellis and brought the sweet scent of honeysuckle. She looked out at the harbor. It was dark, except for lights the length of the pier and ship lanterns at the moorings.

"Okay, courageous heart," she said. "Tomorrow is a new day."

Chapter 19

An Intriguing Story

At the deli, Dorothy saw Bronte taking down her book club notice.

"What's the matter, honey? Didn't things work out?" She was filling the salt-and-pepper shakers along the counter, a dishrag over her shoulder.

Bronte thought about her answer. "Things are working out, Miss Dorothy, but school starts in a few weeks, and we're almost done with the book."

Truth was, they had barely discussed the main character, let alone the plot. "Anyway," Bronte said, "if we keep meeting in September, I'll put up a new announcement with a new title."

"That's logical, honey." Dorothy raised her voice to be heard over the shrill hum of the malt machine. "Sounds like fun."

"Guess that's one way to describe it. There're five of us right now."

"So Willow's been coming? I've known her since she was a baby."

"Yes, she's been coming." Bronte resisted adding, *but I doubt she'll be back*. And no way was Bronte going to say why.

The cashier was a college girl with a ring through her nostril. A squiggly tattoo on her arm was of a spider web. "Excuse me," she said to Bronte. "I couldn't help overhearing. Is Willow's mom any better?"

"Pardon?"

"Well," the girl said, "a few weeks ago I saw out this window that someone was driving her convertible with a person in it all bandaged up. So the next time Willow came in, I asked her. Turns out her mom was being brought home from the hospital. There'd been a terrible accident."

"Really?"

"Yeah," the girl went on. "Her mom went through the windshield of a friend's car, had a ton of stitches. I'm jazzed for her that it wasn't her Mercedes. That baby is such a hot little sports car."

The discussion about Willow's mother now included two other women who were seated at a window table. They carried their burger baskets to the counter to better join the conversation with Dorothy and the cashier.

"Too many martinis," one of them said.

"That's what I heard," said the other.

Bronte waved good-bye, then headed down to the beach. It *was* an intriguing story, but this time she was going to keep her trap shut. If she wanted to know the gory details, she would go directly to Willow.

It was the last Wednesday of July, and crowds from inland had flocked to Gray's Beach to cool off. Even with the ocean breeze, it felt hot.

Lupe and Bronte waited for the other girls on the pier, which was busy with sightseers. Kids were throwing popcorn to the seagulls. Fishermen in folding chairs had a radio by their bait box blaring a baseball game. Meanwhile two mothers with jogging strollers rounded the tip of the pier. They were power-walking, dodging pedestrians as if they were race cars in traffic.

Lupe looked over the railing and said, "Good

thing I didn't bring Sonny Boy. It sure is a long way down. One slip and a girl could plummet to a grisly demise." She grinned at Bronte. "*Plummet*'s an excellent word, don't you think?"

"It's a *delectable* word. Oh good, here comes Jessie. Hi!"

"Hey." Jessie wore sneakers and a small backpack. "I brought some oranges."

"I love oranges!" Bronte and Lupe said in unison.

A whistle caught their attention, and they looked down to the water. Nan was waving up from her dinghy.

Jessie peered over the railing. "You're not serious, are you? We're really going to her boat?"

Lupe was suddenly brave. "Here, I'll go first." She ducked between rails and started her descent, eventually followed by the reluctant Jessie.

At last Bronte saw Willow on the pier, hurrying through a group of Japanese tourists. Bronte stood on her toes to wave to her.

"Willow, hi! I'm so glad you're here."

Willow looked down at the dinghy. Her eyes widened. "You're kidding, right?" The girls were calling up to her, their voices muffled in the wind.

Now Bronte was the confident one. "Nan does this every day. Go ahead, Willow. I'll be right behind you."

Chapter 20

A Private Island

Aboard the *Avalon Rose* the five girls sat in the stern, shaded by a blue canopy. Nan poured them each a cup of water from a plastic jug; then she put Jessie's oranges in a basket so they wouldn't roll around the deck. Her tour of the cabin below had taken one minute, with everyone elbow-to-elbow.

"This is too cool," Lupe said. "Do you ever sleep outside?"

"All the time," said Nan. "When it's not raining Dad takes down the tarp so I can see the stars. It's like being on my own private island."

Bronte seized the moment. "Speaking of islands, what do you guys think about Karana, ultimately?" She had heard this word during a radio interview on NPR and liked how it sounded. "Ultimately," she said again, "do you think Karana's solitude was better than being in society with all its problems?"

"Hmm, maybe," Lupe said. "But how would she know if she was beautiful or not? Without anyone to tell her, she might think she was ugly."

"So?" Willow sounded angry. "It wouldn't matter what you looked like. I think it would be heaven. No one to call you fat, or say you need a nose-job, or that you should wear contacts to make your eyes bluer."

The girls looked over at Willow, but no one responded. Water slapping against the hull sounded louder than ever. So did voices from the beach, of children playing.

Bronte began peeling an orange. Lupe did the same.

Jessie was leaning against a life buoy that hung by the cabin door. She regarded Willow with curiosity, as if she wanted to ask a question.

Finally Nan broke the silence. "Did someone say you need a nose-job?"

After a moment Willow nodded.

"Your nose is darling." Now all the girls were talking.

"Yeah, it's perfect."

"Your eyes are a pretty blue already, and what's wrong with brown eyes or green?"

"You're fantabulous just the way you are."

"Right on."

"Who told you this stuff?"

"My mom, who else?" said Willow. "She's mapped out my life since she failed at hers. I wish my dad were still alive."

Again the girls were quiet.

Willow continued. "Anyway, on an island all alone, you could really be yourself. There'd be no one to put you down or misunderstand things you do."

Bronte was thinking. "*Yeah,*" she said slowly, "but on an island all alone, there'd be no one to palaver with. You could die and no one would miss you. I want someone to miss me."

"Same here," Lupe said. "Besides, it's impossible. There aren't enough islands in the world for every person to go figure things out. We have to try to be ourselves here and now."

Nan jumped onto the bench. "Yoo-hoo! I have an idea. Here. We can practice being ourselves right here. This can be our little island. Want to? My parents said we could keep meeting here if we want."

The girls looked at her with surprise. Even Jessie smiled. Their discussion continued until the ship's bell began chiming.

It was five o'clock. Two hours had flown by like the wind.

The next Wednesday, Bronte's book club met aboard the *Avalon Rose* at two o'clock instead of three.

"Nan, thanks for rowing us out early," said Lupe. Her large sunglasses reflected the faces of the four girls. "We love it here. It's just so—"

"So peaceful," Jessie said, eyes closed. Once again she was sitting by the cabin door, using the life buoy as a backrest.

Bronte opened up her copy of *Blue Dolphins*. "I was wondering if anyone had a chance to read Chapter Sixteen. It's after Karana wounds the dog, then she heals him and names him Rontu—"

"I wish I had a dog." It was Jessie. Her eyes were still closed.

"Me too," said Nan. "But my parents say this boat's too small, even though lots of live-aboards have cats and little terrier types."

Oh, no, thought Bronte, disappointed the topic had changed. *Here we go again.*

Lupe pumped her hands in the air as if cheering. "Guess what, guys. When summer's over my dad says we can get another golden retriever."

"Hey Lupe," said Willow. "Are you going to audition for one of those Purina commercials with Sonny Boy?"

"That's exactly what I'm thinking."

"That's been your dream forever. You'll be perfect."

"I know."

Bronte waved the book in front of the girls. "Speaking of *pets,*" she said. "This part about Karana's dog really got to me. He sits by her and cocks his head, like he's trying to understand what she says."

And before the girls could interrupt, Bronte opened to her bookmark and read: "'I did not know how lonely I had been until I had Rontu to talk to.'"

Bronte looked out at the water. "That's how I

felt," she said. "I mean, when we all first got together, I realized—" She swallowed hard, surprised by the lump in her throat. She sat up straight and brushed her fist across her cheek. "Sorry. I never cry in public."

"It's okay, Bronte."

"I never cry in public, either."

"Same here."

"I only let friends see me cry."

"Right. Friends who *understand* you."

Willow was looking down at her bare feet, but glanced over at Bronte. "Ditto," she said.

Chapter 21

The Cave

The next morning as the sun was burning through the fog, the girls met at the Breakers Café for breakfast. They tied Sonny Boy to the newspaper rack out front then went inside. Dad seated them at a table by the window.

"Okay, bran muffins and guava juice," he said. "Coming right up. And what are you ladies up to this fine day?"

Lupe answered. "Our club is having a field trip to see the caves. Like the ones out on San Nicholas Island."

A fisherman at the next table was stirring cream into his coffee. Without looking up he said, "Two boys drowned there a few years ago. Right below the lighthouse."

Dad glanced over at Mom, who was serving the man a plate of pancakes. She shook her head no.

"Bronte," said her father, "you may go look at the caves, but do not go inside."

The girls hiked from town with Sonny Boy, who trotted beside them with tail wagging. They climbed over the boulders of the breakwater down to the tide pools. The beach here narrowed into a path that curved below Lighthouse Point. Driftwood lined the high watermark.

The lighthouse stood on a point of land that dropped to the sea. Below it at the water's edge were several caves, which gave the base of the cliff a honeycomb appearance. At low tide, some of these could be reached by walking around the point from a secluded cove, the seawater inside just inches deep.

"See that little beach?" Lupe pointed. "We can follow it to the caves. I think we should go *inside* one of them. Like Karana did."

"But is it safe?" Bronte wanted to know. "That fisherman in the café said—"

"Sonny Boy will guide us," Lupe replied. "He's

not afraid of getting his paws wet. Retrievers are natural swimmers."

Jessie crossed her arms. "But he's only a puppy. And I thought we were just coming here to look. Don't you guys remember that Karana gets trapped inside a cave and has to spend the night in her canoe? These things are dangerous when the tide comes in."

"It won't take long," said Lupe.

"We'll be fine," Willow agreed. "It's not such a big deal. What about you, Nan?"

"I'm game. How 'bout you, Bronte?"

"I don't know. My dad said not to." She looked at Nan, then the others. They had eager smiles. "Okay," Bronte said. "I guess so."

The girls observed the half-filled tidal pools. Colorful shells and starfish looked blurry under the water that was ebbing and flowing over them.

"Tide's going out," Lupe said with confidence.

Nan shaded her eyes to see the waves, then she looked down at the pools. "Yeah, I think it is, too."

Jessie walked up to the dry sand. "I'll wait here for you guys. I don't feel adventurous today."

* * *

When the beach dwindled into the rocks, the four girls crab-crawled over them down to the opening of the first cave. It was eight feet wide, and by jumping they could touch the ceiling with their hands. The back wall was far inside with a low archway to another cave.

The water here was ankle deep. Bronte was glad she had worn her sneakers because of the broken shells and pebbles. The girls' voices echoed off the walls dripping from the last wave. As they sloshed their way inside, a surge pushed them toward the rear, knocking them to their knees.

"Nan?" called Bronte. "Lupe? Are you sure the tide's going *out* and not coming *in*?" It worried her that the water was suddenly up to Sonny Boy's belly.

"I think so," answered Nan just as another surge pushed her even farther inside. Under the arch the floor dropped out from under her, and she disappeared. Her hands splashed for the surface.

When Nan caught her breath, she yelled, "It's deep back here. We better get out." Sonny Boy was paddling circles around the girls, whining. He seemed worried.

Bronte's heart thudded in her chest. The water was now up to her waist. She pushed off from the bottom, pulling hard with her arms for the cave's entrance. For every few steps she took, a wave pushed her backward.

All she could think about was getting everyone safely to the cove. Nan was out ahead. Willow had lost her footing and was trying to swim while brushing mats of hair from her eyes. Lupe had drifted to the back of the cave and was hanging onto Sonny Boy's collar.

"Let go of him," Bronte yelled. "You'll drown him."

Lupe wailed, "But I can't swim!"

Chapter 22

Frantic

The cave continued to fill with the rising tide. Bronte tried to reach Lupe, but with each surge their hands slipped out of each other's grasp. It wasn't the moment to ask how anyone could grow up at the beach without learning to swim.

"Guys, take off your shoes!" Bronte shouted. "So they don't drag you down." Salt water stung her eyes as she sunk momentarily, using her hands to pull off her sneakers. Immediately she felt lighter and better able to kick. The surge washed her back and forth inside the cave.

She was terrified for Lupe. And especially for the young dog. His ears were floating out from his yellow head, his mouth open as he struggled to swim with Lupe still clutching his collar. It seemed they were staying in one place.

Bronte still couldn't reach Lupe. She remembered her junior lifesaving class in New Mexico. Her instructor had taken the kids to a river. *Never swim against the tide,* they were taught. *Go with it, aiming for the shore. If you get tired, stop swimming and just float on your back.*

The rocks where they had crawled were now awash and dangerous with sharp edges. But Bronte could see rippling on the surface of the water. It seemed to be a current flowing toward the shelter of the cove.

"Follow me!" she called to her friends. "Just do what I do. Lupe, try to kick!"

Bronte rolled onto her back, stroking into the current. Eventually she felt herself being lifted by a gentle wave that surfed her to safety. Bumping and flailing into her were Nan and Willow. The three girls fell into the wet sand, clinging to each other. Tiny waves washed over their legs as Jessie ran to them.

"Where's Lupe?" she screamed. "Where's Sonny Boy? Where are they?"

The girls were frantic. Valuable minutes were passing, and the tide was coming in, not going out. Bronte had never felt such horror. A friend and her dog were going to drown, and there was nothing they could do about it. Her lifesaving instructor had told stories about kids who had tried to rescue companions, but who ended up drowning themselves.

"It's dangerous to swim back to the cave," she said. "We're too exhausted."

"But we have to do something!" cried Jessie.

Desperate, Bronte looked around her. Lying among the driftwood was a square, flat board that had once been the hatch cover of a sailboat. She picked it up.

"Hey Nan," she called. "I bet this floats. We might be able to reach Lupe in time."

Together they plowed into the water, each with a hand on the board, paddling with the other, kicking as hard as they could.

The hatch cover broke through a cresting wave then bucked the swell behind it. Just as they rounded the rocks below the cliff, they saw two heads, barely on the surface.

"Lupe, we're coming!"

Sonny Boy looked like a seal, he was so dark and wet. His four paws were stirring the green water. "He's not going to make it," Bronte said to Nan. "Look how his head keeps going under."

Lupe's thumb was hooked to his collar, and she was on her back, kicking.

Bronte and Nan finally reached her. "Grab on!" they yelled, and Lupe did, letting go of Sonny Boy's collar. She held onto the wood, resting her chin on the edge.

The girls called for Sonny Boy. "Come on, fella! You can do it! Come on!" But he drifted away from them. They could hear him panting. Bronte wanted to rescue him; but with Lupe hanging on to the board, it was starting to sink. It would take all three of them kicking to keep it afloat.

"Sonny Boy!" Bronte called again. *Oh please don't drown.*

The same current that had earlier floated them into shore now caught them once again. The girls tumbled in the wave, the hatch cover ricocheting into the air. That she surfed in upside down didn't matter to Bronte, nor did the gallon of seawater that rushed up her nose.

All she could think of was Sonny Boy. She

jumped up and down, trying to see over the waves. The girls called for him and whistled; they paced along the beach. But all they saw was the swollen tide.

"Where is he?" Lupe sobbed. "Why was I so stupid?"

Chapter 23

Over the Edge

Bronte shivered with cold. She knew returning to the rough surf could be deadly. But hearing Lupe weep for her lost dog was more than she could bear.

"Nan!" she called. "Let's look over there. Near the cave entrance." She pointed to a cluster of boulders where waves were sloshing.

The girls followed Bronte as she trudged along the high-tide mark, cluttered with flotsam and drift-wood. Soon they could see down to where they had found Lupe.

"There he is!" Nan cried. "He's still there!"

Sonny Boy was frantically pawing the rock, trying to climb up, but he kept slipping back into the water. Every time his head went under, it took longer for him to surface.

Bronte got down on her stomach and stretched out her arm. "I can almost reach him! Nan, sit on my legs so I don't fall in!"

But just as Bronte touched his collar, the surge pulled Sonny Boy from her grasp. Foam washed over his head. He was sinking.

Lupe cried, "Don't give up, Bronte! Please keep trying!"

Then Bronte remembered the yellow rope she'd seen the other day among the driftwood. She yelled so the others could find it. "But hurry! I'm slipping in. Nan, stay on my feet!"

Instantly Bronte felt several hands on her ankles. Again she stretched her arms down into the water and this time was able to touch the dog's ear. Now he pawed furiously, trying to reach her. He raised his head for another breath.

"Come on, boy! I almost had you!" Bronte could feel her knees scrape against the boulder as her friends held her down. Her arms and neck ached from the strain. But a few seconds later, a wave pushed him close enough that she was able to grab the scruff of his neck.

"Got 'im!" she cried.

He was breathing hard. The whites of his eyes were huge.

Then Bronte felt the slap of the rope against her shoulder. Memories from Girl Scouts and life-saving helped her think quickly. She tied a loose knot.

"Hang on to the rope!" she yelled to her friends. "And hang on to *me*. He's really heavy."

Another surge pulled Sonny Boy away, but Bronte had such a firm hold, he merely floated. His brown eyes met hers.

"Don't worry, boy. We're gonna get you out."

Now holding him with one hand, she slipped the noose over his shoulders and front paws, tightening it against his chest.

"Pull!" she screamed.

And while some hands held Bronte's legs, others tugged on the rope. With the help of one more wave, Sonny Boy was on dry ground.

The girls petted him and checked for injuries as he shook out his fur, soaking them. Then he retched up all the salt water he had swallowed. Again he shook his fur.

Bronte broke down crying. She hugged his

soggy neck. "Sonny Boy, I'm so sorry. We should never have gone into that cave."

Their walk in bare feet over the stones into town was slow. All but Jessie had lost their shoes. They kept studying Sonny Boy to make sure he wasn't limping.

"Think he'll be okay?" the girls asked one another.

Just then the golden retriever stopped. He had spotted a cluster of seagulls perched in the sand, looking out at the ocean. He lowered his head and lifted a front paw in the pointing position. For one quivery moment he stared at the gulls; then he burst into a run, scattering them to the wind.

Lupe laughed. "Well, I guess that answers our question."

Chapter 24

Salt Water Heals

The harbor swell rocked the *Avalon Rose* where the five girls were gathered. They were still shaken by the near-drownings of the day before. At Nan's invitation they had met on the pier with sack lunches and were now sitting together on the boat's bow. The sky was blue, and the water sparkled with sunshine. It was a perfect summer day, but no one had worn a bathing suit.

"Did you tell your parents what happened?" they asked one another.

"No way."

"Me neither."

"Never."

Willow said, "My mom would love a reason to forbid me from hanging out with Bronte."

"But it's not Bronte's fault," said Lupe. "It was my idea."

"Yeah, but we all went along with it."

"Except Jessie."

They looked over at her. Her dark hair lay over her shoulders, and she was leaning against the mast, by the pot of geraniums. "I was so freaked out," she said. "I kept watching and waiting and worrying. It reminded me—" Jessie didn't finish her sentence. She shook her head.

"What?" they asked.

"Nothing."

"Jessie, what did it remind you of?"

"Nothing, I said!"

"Okay, sorry."

Eager to change the subject, Bronte said, "My parents asked how I skinned my knees. If they knew I disobeyed them, they'd be furious. So I told them, on the rocks, but not the whole story. Told them my bloody shoulder was from body surfing. That I scraped against the sand when I was coming in."

"Which is true," said Nan. "That's how my elbow got wrecked." She bent her arm to show the abrasion. "But the salt water helps a lot. It's already getting better. I went swimming this morning."

"Hey!" cried Lupe. "That totally reminds me of something Karana said. Remember when she found the wounded otter and took care of it but decided not to use her herbal ointment? She said the otter would be okay because 'salt water heals.'"

"Yeah."

Nan was standing in the bowsprit, which had a waist-high rail extending over the water. "Look over there, guys." She pointed to one of the large harbor buoys. It was red-and-white striped with a speed-limit sign on top: 5 MPH. It was anchored; but as it rolled from the current, the base of it tipped low enough into the water for a sea lion to slide up onto its rim, where three others were already sunning themselves.

"Now every time I watch those seals," Nan said, "or the dolphins that come into the bay, I always think of Karana. She loved animals so much. They were her friends. I bet if she were a modern girl, she would become a marine biologist, like what I want to be. Remember what she said about animals? I even underlined it in my book. 'Without them the earth would be an unhappy place.'"

"Totally," Bronte and Willow agreed.

Suddenly Lupe's eyes filled with tears. She coughed, trying not to cry. "I'm so glad I have Sonny Boy."

Bronte leaned back against a cushion. They were discussing *Island of the Blue Dolphins*, and it wasn't even a book club meeting. And it had happened all on its own.

Jessie, however, had fallen silent. Her head was down, arms wrapped around her knees.

Chapter 25

And the Sea
Was Empty

Bronte was relieved they weren't in her sunroom where Jessie might run from the house. Those meetings had often felt awkward to her. But today on the bow of the *Avalon Rose*, things were different.

No one was trying to get off this little island.

"Are you okay, Jessie?" Bronte asked.

Jessie lifted her head and brushed her dark hair away from her face. She was pale.

"Is it the boat?" Nan asked. "I have some seasick pills down below."

Jessie shook her head. "No, it's not that."

The girls waited. Meanwhile a noisy flock of gulls passed overhead as a fishing boat motored by, its engine at a slow putter. Its wake caused the *Avalon Rose* to pitch.

Jessie kept her eyes down. "I haven't told anyone why we moved to Gray's Beach."

The girls were quiet.

"Okay." Jessie took a deep breath. "In the first chapters of our book, remember when Kimki canoes away from the island? The tribe hopes he'll return with a ship from the mainland to rescue them. Remember that part?"

"Yes," the girls answered. Even Willow nodded.

"Well, there's a part in there I can't get out of my head. The tribe waited and watched for months. 'But the spring came and went and the sea was empty.' They never saw Kimki again. Those words—*and the sea was empty*—they really get to me."

Jessie looked out at the buoy. The seals had begun a ruckus with loud barking. Then one by one they slid into the water, their flippers swirling the surface. She gazed after them for a moment, then her eyes filled with tears.

"Three years ago my brother, Tommy—he was seventeen—well, he and my parents had a really bad fight. They took away the car keys because he got three Ds on his report card, which ruined their Ivy League plans for him. It was horrible, the things they said to each other. One thing led to another. He punched a hole in our kitchen wall; then my mom shoved him out the front door. She screamed at him to never come back. But she didn't mean it."

Jessie started to cry.

Nan went belowdecks and returned with a roll of toilet paper, which she handed to Jessie. "We're out of Kleenex. Sorry."

Bronte had a tight feeling in her chest. She was afraid to hear this story about Tommy.

Jessie wiped her cheeks. "Anyway, we lived by the harbor in Redondo Beach, and our boat was in one of the slips there. You had to have a key for the dock, to get in the gate. *Waltzing Matilda*— that was her name—she was only twenty-three feet long so she was easy to handle, and Tommy had been sailing since he was a little kid. But during their fight my parents hid the harbor key." Jessie was still hugging her knees. Her lip quivered.

"But *I* knew where the spare was. I sneaked it outside to Tommy so he wouldn't have to sleep on the streets. I was only ten. I wanted to help my big brother. I was sure he'd come back and take me sailing like he did every weekend."

Here Jessie broke into deep sobs. Her shoulders shook. Willow and Lupe crawled over the coiled ropes on deck to sit next to her. Nan placed her hand on Jessie's arm. Bronte also scooted close. She laid her cheek against the girl's heaving back and hugged her tight.

Once Jessie started to cry, she couldn't stop. Ten minutes passed before she was able to speak. Her voice was hoarse. Each girl handed her a wad of tissue.

"Thanks," she said. After wiping her eyes, she continued. "So Tommy never called or sent word to say where he went. Never. On his eighteenth birthday Mom and Dad drove down to San Diego because a friend saw someone who looked like him in the harbor. I was only eleven, but they left me alone. Now they spend all their time trying to find him, and they act like I don't exist. My mother says that if I hadn't been so stupid, Tommy would be at Yale or Harvard right now. He was supposed to become a lawyer and make our family proud.

"That's why they pushed me into this book club, so I'd be ready to take his place at some stupid college. It's so lame."

Jessie shook her head, her eyes again filling with tears. Nan offered another wad of toilet paper. The others pressed close to her in silent sympathy.

The girls sat aboard the *Avalon Rose* all afternoon. The harbor was choppy from skiffs and outboard dinghies coming and going. The breeze brought the smell of diesel fuel from a tourist boat heading beyond the breakwater. Bronte loved it out here. She loved feeling relaxed with her new friends, though she was upset by Jessie's story. They were passing around cookies from their lunches and a large bag of tortilla chips.

"I'd like to take you guys to the lighthouse," Jessie said. "The keeper is a family friend. My dad moved us to Gray's Beach so he could climb the tower and watch the ocean. He hopes he'll see Tommy aboard the *Waltzing Matilda*, sailing in the channel. I personally think Daddy is losing it. He and Mom hardly ever talk anymore, and I don't remember the last time we all had dinner together. I can't stand how quiet eveyone is. I can't stand that everything's my fault."

"No, it is *not!*" Lupe said. "Your parents need counseling." The others agreed.

"Jessie, your brother took the boat out, not you."

"Yeah."

"Besides, he could've climbed over the fence on his own, or another sailor would've opened the gate for him."

"He'll come back when he's ready. It's not your fault, Jess."

Jessie began to cry again. From the roll of toilet paper, she unraveled a length of tissue and held it to her eyes. After a moment she looked at the girls.

"You'll love it when we get to the top of the lighthouse. You can see for miles and miles. The islands are brown bumps. I've seen schools of dolphins and orcas. In the fall we saw the gray whales swimming south for Mexico; then in the spring they swam back with their babies. I see so many interesting things, but"—Jessie wiped her eyes—"but my father only sees an empty ocean."

Chapter 26

A Secret

Bronte and Willow were walking to the beach. Stores along the strand had signs in their windows: BACK-TO-SCHOOL SPECIALS.

"I can't believe summer's almost over," Bronte said.

"Ditto," said Willow. "It'll be torture sitting in class when you can look out at perfect waves. The weather is so awesome in September. Actually school is torture all year long."

"Really? What about English?" Bronte paused. "Is reading fun for you?"

Willow's sunglasses reflected blue ocean. "You mean, honestly?" she asked.

"Yeah. Honestly. Do you like to read?"

"No." Willow pulled the elastic from her ponytail and shook her hair in the wind. "Reading is hard. I'm so slow, I feel stupid. But my sister says to keep trying and that if I read *something* every day, it'll get easier, like starting a new good habit. I joined the book club so I could practice with girls my own age and make friends. *Plus*"—Willow grinned at Bronte—"it really ticks my mom off."

The girls spread their towels in the sand by the lifeguard tower. When the guard saw Willow, he stood and stretched. Ever so slightly he sucked in his stomach and flexed his biceps.

"Hello there, gals!" he called down to them. "Awesome day, huh?"

"Hi Jake." Willow waved to him then turned to Bronte. "Our moms work in the same real-estate office."

Bronte took off her T-shirt, then squirted sunscreen over her arms. She felt like a Humvee next to her friend in the bikini.

"Hey Willow?" she said softly. "I can help you read better. It'll be fun. And your sister's right. The more you practice, the better you get." Bronte was surprised at her boldness and even more surprised by her friend's answer.

"When can we start?"

Bronte laughed. "Want to come to my house after the beach?"

"Yeah, but I can't today. Gotta pick up a prescription for my mom and take it to her work."

"Is she sick?"

"No. Well, sorta. She needs antibiotics again. Some of her stitches got infected from makeup."

"From the car accident?" Bronte asked.

"How'd you find out?"

"At the deli they said your mom went through the windshield. It must have been awful."

"Oh, she'll be fine. Hey, let's go for a swim! It's getting hot." Willow took off her sunglasses and slipped them into her bag.

They dove under a wave. When they came up and were treading water, Willow called to Bronte. "Want to know the truth?"

"About what?"

"My mom's accident?"

"Sure."

"But you can't tell anyone, okay?"

"Willow, I'm a veritable secret-keeper."

"What does *veritable* mean anyway? You're always using big words."

"It means truly or actually."

"Then why don't you just say that?"

"'Cause sometimes fancy words are more fun than regular ones."

"Okay. Whatever."

A breaking wave was rushing toward them. Bronte ducked under the foam until it had rumbled overhead. After counting eight long seconds, she popped to the surface and gasped for air.

"Willow!" she yelled above the churning water. "What's the secret?"

"It wasn't an accident, Bronte. It was a makeover! She had a face-lift and a boob job. And *next* she wants her plastic surgeon to straighten my nose."

Chapter 27

Always Watching

The next day, Jessie led the girls on a field trip to the lighthouse. The staircase inside the lighthouse spiraled upward, its metal steps clanking from the girls' shoes as they climbed to the top. Bronte clung to the rail that was bolted to the stone walls. The height was frightening.

"Just don't look down," Jessie had instructed them. "Keep looking out at the ocean. It's sort of like being in an airplane, as long as you don't think about how far up we are."

Jessie was cheerful today. Her hair was in a ponytail with a bright yellow scrunchie, and color had come to her cheeks.

"Wait till you see how far apart the islands are," she said. "No wonder Karana stayed on San

Nicholas for eighteen years and didn't canoe to the mainland. This channel is one of the roughest in the world. Right, Mr. Frank?"

"That's right, Jess."

The lighthouse keeper looked like a camp counselor, young enough to be in college. His T-shirt said WEST COAST MARATHON, and he wore an LA Dodgers baseball cap.

"Take your time," he told the girls. "You can stand outside on the platform if you want, but be careful. Last year a couple junior-high boys started horsing around out there, and one of them took a nasty spill." Mr. Frank stood on a stepladder to polish the glass sides of the lantern.

The girls exchanged nervous glances.

"So . . . what . . . happened?" Nan asked.

"Hmm, you might say he'll never do *that* again."

"Did he . . . die?"

He looked over his shoulder at them, cloth in hand. "Nope. I wasn't going to let him fall. Grabbed him by the seat of his pants just in time. He dangled a bit till I pulled him up. Poor kid. He was shaking like a scared poodle. Go ahead, just open the latch there."

Again the girls looked at one another. Suddenly Bronte felt brave. She stepped over the threshold leading outside. The wind was fierce. She could feel it pushing her. It whistled through the grate beneath her feet, billowing her T-shirt and her hair. For one terrifying moment she could picture herself being blown over the ledge and plummeting to a bloody death. Her poor parents! Immediately she stepped back inside, her heart racing.

The others stayed where they were.

The lookout room was a circle of tall windows. A hole in the floor dropped to the ground many stories below. Bronte glanced over the protective rail, down into a dizzying coil of steps. She made herself turn away.

From that height the harbor looked like a bathtub crowded with toy boats. The ocean was a panorama of blue, dotted with whitecaps from the wind. Bronte recognized Santa Cruz Island and saw other isles, in the haze.

"Girls, look out there," said Mr. Frank, pointing to an elegant sailing ship. Its masts were full of white sails. "That's the *Lady Washington*. You probably saw *Curse of the Black Pearl—*"

"Yeah!"

"Johnny Depp!"

"He's so hot!"

"He's fantabulous!"

Mr. Frank laughed. "Then you'll appreciate that the *Lady Washington* played the *HMS Interceptor* in the film. She's a genuine Hollywood star. In real life, schools use her to teach kids about the ocean and sailing. Pretty cool, huh?"

"Wow."

The lighthouse keeper tucked his cloth in his back pocket, then put a pair of binoculars to his eyes. Slowly he scanned the wide view of the ocean, turning north then south.

"See anything, Mr. Frank?" Jessie asked.

"Same as yesterday, Jess. Couple oil tankers, some scuba divers heading out."

Lupe asked if he would be able to spot a tiny sailboat from this distance.

"I'm always watching," he answered, "and I know what to look for. If Tommy ever sails by on the *Waltzing Matilda*, you bet I'll see 'im."

Chapter 28

Making Plans

The girls were walking back from the lighthouse along the beach, discussing their last week of summer vacation.

"How about a sleepover?" Nan suggested. "I wish we could have it on the boat, but there's not enough room for all of us. My parents would be flummoxed by all the commotion."

"And at my house my little brothers would spy on us," said Lupe.

Willow was dragging her foot in the wet sand, making a long line behind them, which scuffed her red toenail polish. She laughed. "Well, there goes the pedicure. Anyway, sorry guys, but an all-nighter at my place would be a veritable downer. My mom would lecture us about beauty and fashion. You would leave the next morning feeling like gargoyles."

"And we can't go to *my* house," said Jessie. "My parents are too sad. I'm embarrassed to have anyone over. Bronte's is the best place."

"Yeah!"

When an incoming wave splashed against their knees, they scattered up to dry ground like sandpipers. Except Bronte. Exhilarated that the book club wanted to spend the night at *her* house, she threw up her arms and let herself fall into the surf. She lay in the water, letting the foam wash over her, savoring the tingle of salt water on her skin.

"Hey, what're you doing, Quirky Girl?" Willow shouted.

Bronte felt giddy. Even though she would be starting a brand new school, she already had four friends. Real friends. They had been mad at each other, they had cried together, and they had laughed together. She jumped up, hair dripping in her face. Her T-shirt was plastered to her chest.

"We can camp out in my sunroom," she said. "I'm sure my parents will say it's okay. But there's one condition."

"What is it?"

"Sonny Boy comes, too."

"But he's a dog."

"Precisely," said Bronte. "Remember what Karana said about all the birds and otters and dolphins?"

Lupe threw her arm wide in a dramatic pose. She shouted into the wind, "'Without animals, the earth would be a miserable place.'"

As the girls continued home from their field trip, they branched off in separate directions. Lupe was going to help her father in the bakery; Jessie and Nan both had afternoon babysitting jobs.

"So what're you guys doing for the rest of the day?" they asked Willow and Bronte as they headed up the hill.

"First I'm changing into some dry clothes," Bronte said. "Then we're making cookies for my parents' housewarming party."

"Cool."

"Maybe see you at the beach tomorrow?"

"Definitely."

"Okay."

"Later."

*   *   *

Bronte tied on a white chef's apron and put on a tall white chef's hat. Then she opened her favorite cookbook to oatmeal butterscotch bars and set it on the counter. The pages were glossy with colored photos, and the recipes were printed in large type.

"Start right here," she said to Willow, who was wearing a checkered apron. "Read me the first line, and I'll get what we need from the fridge or wherever. Then when everything's out, we'll start measuring and mixing. Ready?"

"Ready. 'Two cups plus two tablespoons unbleached all-purpose flour.'"

Bronte stepped on a stool and reached into a cupboard. "Flour. Got it. Next?"

"'Seven tablespoons of packed light brown sugar.'"

"Got it."

Willow continued to read slowly, careful to pronounce each word, as Bronte set out the ingredients.

"'One cup butterscotch chips.' Oh I love these. Mind if I have some, Bronte?"

"Grab a handful. Here, me too. This is the best part, but aren't you on a diet?"

"Nope. Not today. My gluteus maximus is just fine. You know, Bronte, I had to ask my brainiac sister what that meant."

Bronte beamed.

Willow continued. "'One cup chocolate chips.' Yum. Want some of these, too?"

"Veritably, yes."

"'Two cups of quick-cooking rolled oats.'"

"Oats. Got 'em. Hey Willow?"

"Yeah?"

"Are you having fun yet? Reading, I mean?"

"Reading?" Willow started to laugh. She patted Bronte's chef's hat until it poofed down over her eyes. "I guess I am, Quirky Girl."

Chapter 29

Party Dog

Bronte's friends arrived at five o'clock in the afternoon.

After barbecuing hot dogs and hamburgers, the girls set up camp in the sunroom. Soon there was a cozy clutter of blankets, sleeping bags, and pillows. Sonny Boy lounged in the center, one paw folded under his chest. He was dressed up for the party with a purple bandanna that matched Lupe's capris and head scarf. His eyes were on a bowl of potato chips that had been left unattended.

Bronte rolled in a cart with a rented TV and DVD player. "We checked out seven movies from the library. One is my all-time favorite: *Amadeus*. It's historical, about Mozart."

"Oh, please."

"Okay, how about *High School Musical*?"

"Come on, Bronte. We've seen that, like, five times."

"Yeah."

"What else did you get?"

Bronte read the other titles. Last was *Island of the Blue Dolphins*. "I thought it would round out our summer together."

"Hey, that's not a bad idea," said Nan. "How about we start with our old friend Karana?"

A snuffling, crackling sound drew their attention to the other side of the room where Sonny Boy was helping himself to the chips. Before anyone could grab the bowl from him, he had licked it clean. He was as calm and pleased, as if finishing his own dinner.

Lupe said, "Bad dog! You bamboozled us!" In response to her voice, he wagged his tail and lifted his front paw to shake. He didn't seem to think he was in trouble.

"Hey, where's the rest of my hot dog?" Nan asked. "It was here a minute ago."

Willow picked up an empty paper plate. It was gooey. "Probably the same place where my burger went. I only ate half."

The girls looked at Sonny Boy, then at their hostess to see if she was upset. But Bronte laughed out loud. "What's a party without a dog to help clean up?"

"But what if he upchucks?"

"Oh guys, this is *nothing*." Lupe waved her hand. "You should see what my little brothers feed him under the table. He *loves* enchiladas. Once he ate a taco salad with salsa and guacamole. My dad set it on a patio bench to check the barbecue, and when he came back, Sonny Boy had eaten the whole thing. He didn't even barf."

The girls giggled.

"I want a dog," Jessie reminded everyone.

"Me too."

"No matter what kind I get, Rontu is going to be his name."

"Same here."

Bronte kneeled beside Sonny Boy. As she scratched under his chin, he gave her a slurpy kiss.

"Eeeew," said the girls.

"Gross."

"Yuck! Canine halitosis."

But Bronte didn't care. She hugged him. "You can come to my house anytime, boy."

Chapter 30

Little Women

The last movie ended at three o'clock in the morning. Bronte turned off the TV and rolled it to the hallway, then returned to the floor with her friends. She could hear the surf through the open windows of the sunroom, even though the others were talking. She lay down on her quilt and closed her eyes. Though tired, she did not want to sleep.

Bronte listened to the girls. Already it was the end of August. She wondered if their book club would keep meeting during the school year and if there would be further spats or misunderstandings.

At least we're off to a good start.

Hungry, she went into the kitchen and flicked on a light. She took a quart of ice cream from the freezer, spoons and a scooper from a drawer, then from the cupboard she got five bowls, a jar of hot-fudge sauce—which she microwaved—also a can of whipped cream and some napkins.

"Who wants dessert?" she asked, carrying a tray from the kitchen.

It was nearly four o'clock when they finished their sundaes. Willow and Jessie gathered up the bowls and rinsed them in the kitchen sink so Sonny Boy couldn't find them. He was sacked out on Lupe's sleeping bag. Sunrise was just two hours away.

Bronte turned out the lights, except for a small ship's lamp by the fireplace, which gave the room a cozy glow. The girls curled up in their bedding. The sugar and chocolate had perked them up, reviving their conversations; but Bronte noticed the silences were getting longer. Soon a quiet snoring came from one of the pillows.

Just when Bronte dropped into a deep sleep, a voice woke her.

"And you know what else?" Nan said.

"Mmm?"

"Narwhals have a long ivory tusk, about six feet long, like unicorns. It's actually an overgrown tooth and is usually covered with algae, except for the tip."

"Hey, wait a minute." Jessie was awake now. "That's very nice about narwhals," she said, "but unicorns are just fantasy. They're not real."

"But maybe long ago they *were* real," said Willow. "And"—she yawned, covering her mouth with the back of her hand—"and anyway, maybe that's where the legend started. My sister says that dinosaurs are mentioned in the Bible and so is an animal that breathed fire."

Now Lupe joined the discussion. "Archaeologists have found bones of dinosaurs, but no unicorns that I've heard of."

Bronte snuggled under her quilt to listen.

She was thinking about *Island of the Blue Dolphins*, the last chapter, where the ship sails to San Nicholas Island to rescue the Indian girl. When one of the men talks to Karana, she can't understand him; but she is amazed by the sound of his words. After being alone for so many years, she finds that the human voice is a comfort. "There is no sound like this in all the world," Karana says at the end of her story.

Bronte listened to her friends laughing and debating, and she thought, *Yes, it is true. Veritably true.*

How to Start a Book Club

1. Gather a few friends or acquaintances who like to read. Small groups of four to eight are easier to manage because you don't have to shout to be heard.

2. Pick a leader. This helps when there's a runaway talker or when people soar off the subject. The leader needs to know how to clear the throat ("Ahem!") and tap a pencil on the table to get people's attention.

3. Pick a meeting place, preferably where food is allowed. Refreshments are a must for a

convivial gathering! Try the recipe for *Bronte's Brownies* in the back of this book.

4. Decide how often you want to meet. Bronte's club met every week because it was during the summer, but once a month is standard. This gives everyone time to read.

5. Start on time and end on time. An hour is good, two can get draggy. Ninety minutes allows for wild off-topic maneuvers.

6. Choose a book together. Public libraries are great for providing lists of their multiple titles. This way everyone in your group can check out a copy without having to buy one.

7. Some readers might like to prepare a list of questions to discuss; others might prefer to wing it and see what happens.

8. Be polite and enjoy one another's company.

9. In the author's experience, dogs are a

welcome addition to book clubs. They're good listeners, they clean up spilled snacks, and they don't use cell phones.

10. Have fun!

Bronte's Brownies

INGREDIENTS:

1 box brownie mix (19 to 21 oz. size)

2 eggs

2 tablespoons vegetable oil

3/4 cup applesauce

1 cup miniature marshmallows

6 oz. (one small package) semi-sweet chocolate chips or butterscotch chips or white chocolate chips or a combination of the three

Optional: 1/2 cup chopped pecans or almonds

DIRECTIONS:

1. Preheat oven to 350 degrees. Grease a 9x13 inch pan.
2. In a large bowl, combine the brownie mix, eggs, oil, and applesauce. Stir with a large spoon about 50 strokes until blended so that no dry powder is sticking to the bowl.
3. Now add the marshmallows, chocolate chips, nuts, or whatever combination you have in the

kitchen. Don't smash it around; just stir until blended evenly.

4. Pour into pan, spreading the batter to the edges with a spoon or spatula.
5. Bake for 30 to 35 minutes. Watch for the brownies to just start pulling away from the side of the pan. Poke a toothpick into the center, and if it comes out dry, your brownies are done.

SUGGESTIONS:

1. Let the brownies cool for one hour before cutting.
2. While you're waiting, wipe down the kitchen counter and clean up any mess.
3. These brownies are an excellent book club snack and can be served on a napkin (to save washing dishes). They taste best when shared with friends.

ACKNOWLEDGMENTS

Special thanks to my young book club friends in Boise, Idaho, who were the inspiration for Bronte's story, and to teen reader Jourdan R. Delbridge. Thank you also to my grown-up book club friend, Edwina, who helped test and taste recipes for *Bronte's Brownies*, and to her youthful neighborhood crew who gave the final thumbs up.

Most especially, I'm grateful to be reunited with my long ago editor, Regina Griffin, and for editorial direction from Mary Cash and Leanna Petronella.